A Politically Correct Dictionary and Guide

DR KEVIN DONNELLY
Illustrated by Johannes Leak

Connor Court Publishing

Published in 2019 by Connor Court Publishing Pty Ltd

Copyright © Kevin Donnelly (text), Johannes Leak (illustrations)

All rights reserved. No part of this book may be reproduced or transmitted in any form or by any means, electronic or mechanical, including photocopying, recording or by any information storage and retrieval system, without prior permission in writing from the publisher.

Connor Court Publishing Pty Ltd
PO Box 7257
Redland Bay QLD 4165
sales@connorcourt.com
Phone 0497-900-685

www.connorcourtpublishing.com.au

Printed in Australia

ISBN: 978-1-925826-72-2

Cover design: Maria Giordano

Front Cover Cartoon by Johannes Leak

Printed and Bound in Australia

Political correctness is the antithesis of education. Education is about opening the mind and encouraging thought and that will sometimes include ideas which might be characterised as dangerous. Notions of political correctness are about corralling thought and banishing ideas which don't fit prevailing prejudices and ideologies. Political correctness has no place in beneficial education.

-- Alan Jones – Radio and TV commentator and journalist.

This pithy dictionary records a campaign to lasso or strangle the language. In the process, the campaign often falsifies the past or present.

-- Geoffrey Blainey – Historian.

Kevin Donnelly has frequently railed against the dangers of political correctness. This work commendably highlights its stultifying effect on plain speaking. Not everyone will identify with all of the examples he cites, but the volume is a useful contribution to a better understanding of how simple, direct language has been undermined.

-- John Howard – Australian Prime Minister.

I spend hours, days and weeks at my laptop, working on stories where I have to find exactly the right phrase and progression of thought in words to convey, with accuracy but also originality, what I am seeing in my mind, and feeling in my emotions, to my reader. It's the duck paddling seemingly effortlessly but with a huge amount of activity under the water. Now that is even harder to do these days - sometimes it feels impossibly hard - as I duck and weave around the PC monitor in my brain …Kevin Donnelly precisely and chillingly depicts what is happening to language and thought under PC regulation and the dangerous history behind it. Read his arguments and be galvanised.

-- Shelley Gare – Commentator and journalist.

An essential guide to the most dangerous intellectual disease of our time.

-- Tony Abbott – Australian Prime Minister.

Dr Kevin Donnelly is one of the best friends two generations of young Australians have had. He is a tireless advocate for educational quality and understands what makes a difference. His insights and experience make this book another winner.
Tess Livingstone – Journalist at *The Australian* **and author.**

Kevin Donnelly is the best thinker and writer in Australia on issues of children's education and how political correctness is enforcing group think and destroying the language. He has, in the 25 years since I first published his work, been rigorous in outing the effects of faddish left wing approaches to teacher training and educational theory that have so damaged our school system.

Chris Mitchell – Past editor of *The Australian* **and journalist.**

Dedicated to Bill Leak: inspired cartoonist and cultural warrior.
1956-2017

CONTENTS

Foreword   1

Introduction   6

Politically correct and incorrect words and expressions   15

Political correctness and the cultural-left's long march through the institutions   101

Political correctness: No longer a laughing matter   102

The past is a foreign country   113

The imposition of politically correct language and group think   121

The brave new world of political correctness   129

Political correctness and its impact on schools   136

Political correctness and its impact on universities   150

Radical gender and sexuality theory   155

What's to be done   159

Dr Kevin Donnelly AM

Since first warning about the dangers of political correctness during the early 90s Kevin has established a reputation as one of Australia's leading conservative commentators and authors fighting against the cultural-left ideology and group think that is poisoning society and stifling free and open debate.

Political correctness denies the ability to reason and to be impartial as knowledge, supposedly, is a social construct and all relationships are based on privilege and power. In opposition Kevin champions the strengths and benefits of Western civilisation and a liberal education dedicated to what the poet T. S. Eliot describes as "the preservation of learning, for the pursuit of truth, and in so far as men are capable of it, the attainment of wisdom".

Kevin also champions the West's Judeo-Christian heritage and on-going traditions that underpin our political and legal systems and way of life and that are being undermined by what Sydney's Archbishop Fisher describes as "absolutist secularism" and a rainbow alliance of neo-Marxist, postmodern theories.

As well as appearing on Sky News Kevin is a commentator for The Australian newspaper and writes regularly for The Herald Sun, The Daily Telegraph, Quadrant Online and the Australian Spectator. Previous publications include: *Why our schools are failing, Dumbing Down, Australia's Education Revolution, Educating your child: it's not rocket science, Taming the black dog, The Culture of Freedom, How political Correctness Is Destroying Australia* and *How Political Correctness Is Destroying Education.*

Kevin taught English and Humanities for 18 years in Victorian government and non-government secondary schools and has also been a member of state and national curriculum bodies, including: the Victorian Board of Studies and the federally funded Discovering Democracy Programme. After completing a number of projects benchmarking state and territory curriculum syllabuses and frameworks internationally in 2014 Kevin co-chaired the review of the Australian National Curriculum for the Commonwealth Government.

He is a Senior Research Fellow at the Australian Catholic University and Director of the Education Standards Institute. In the 2016 Queen's Birthday Honours List Dr Donnelly was appointed as a Member of the Order of Australia for services to education. Kevin can be contacted via email at kevind@netspace.net.au or his website kevindonnelly.com.au.

FOREWORD

With his third book-length polemic against political correctness in just over a year, Dr Kevin Donnelly is on a veritable crusade against what he thinks is poisoning our teaching institutions, weakening our economy, and even sapping our ability to think clearly.

Donnelly, a teacher, academic, and former reviewer of the national curriculum for the Abbott government, is a rare and forthright warrior for common sense in a world where it's more desperately needed than ever. For those that think political correctness is frustrating to the speech of old (terms such as 'mankind') but essentially harmless, think again. As Donnelly says, this is "more than just being civil, treating all with respect and basing one's beliefs and arguments on logic and reason". Political correctness is insidious; by its very nature, the way it has stealthily crept into our language and through our institutions and now corporations, it is, he argues "a form of group think and language control used by the cultural-left to enforce its ideology on individuals and society more broadly".

The problem, that Donnelly thinks is fast becoming a crisis, is that the predominant ethos among educators is that all cultures are equal (except our own) and that all people need to be treated with great deference (unless they're conservative, white, or male, in which case they're liable to receive relentless criticism and mockery). He quotes President Abraham Lincoln to the effect that the philosophy of the classroom today is the philosophy of government a generation later.

Rather than engage in the battle of ideas, openly and with the use of argument and fact, activists on the left have worked out that shutting down debate is far more effective when shaping the minds of the young. After all, it was the former Victorian premier and education minister Joan Kirner who said at a 1983 Fabian Society meeting that "we have to reshape education so that it is part of the socialist struggle for equality, participation, and social change, rather than an instrument for the capitalist system".

And haven't they been successful.

As Donnelly writes, "criticise multiculturalism or immigration and you are racist, xenophobic and a white supremacist, suggest that it's normal for children to be either boys and girls and that the love between a woman and a man should be celebrated and you are homophobic, transphobic and guilty of heteronormativity. Defend Christianity and you are a god-botherer and a paedophile and defend Western civilisation you are labelled as Eurocentric and guilty of whiteness and oppressing so-called victim groups".

What has thus far escaped most people's attention, even now, is the extent to which our institutions have capitulated. The 'long march of the left through the institutions' has been under way since the 1960s. As the conservative British MP and thinker Michael Gove put it, Marxism was revised "as primarily a cultural rather than an economic movement. In place of anger directed at traditional capitalism, scorn was directed at the reigning values of the West". It's this that Donnelly is trying to alert us to, while we still have the capacity to understand the challenge and to resist it.

Invariably, the cultural left appeals to our most decent instincts, in its attempts to weaken us. It pushes for the open borders that weaken our societies on grounds of compassion for refugees. It pushes the climate change policies that weaken our economies under the guise of saving the planet. It pushes gender fluidity to weaken family ties in the name of inclusion for our most vulnerable fellow human beings. Compassion, conservation and inclusion are, of course, all worthy drivers of policy but not to the point of compromising the strength and cohesion of the only societies which actually exhibit these fine traits; countries in the West, like our own.

Donnelly's latest work is full of telling examples of the cultural self-doubt that we need to recognise and resist. Why, for instance, is the Australian Curriculum and Reporting Authority arguing that "indigenous science" be taught at all levels in school science classes when, as the indigenous leader Warren Mundine points out, "science is simply science regardless of ethnicity and race"? Why have we dropped the terms AD (anno domini) and BC (before Christ) in favour of CE (common era) and BCE (before the common era), even though we are actually dating things from the supposed time of Jesus' birth? Why are we squeamish about Australia Day even though the proclamation of the colony marked the beginning of modern Australia (with, eventually, much higher living standards and properly recognised rights for Aboriginal people too)?

Why are the most strident feminists invariably so slow to acknowledge the crimes against women committed in the name of Islam? Why is the Australian Public Service Commission choosing to warn against "unintended discrimination" through "unconscious bias" at a time when close to half of all departmental heads are now female?

If we are on the verge of being out-competed economically by China, out-muscled militarily by the new dictators in Beijing and the Kremlin, and out-believed by Muslim fundamentalism – as it sometimes seems these days – it might well be our very "kindness" that's been the West's undoing. We don't stand up for ourselves, our values and our way of life lest it upset someone who might have been hardly done by or is otherwise felt to be more morally deserving. At one level, it's to our great credit that we're always prepared to look at things from another's perspective and to bend over in order to be fair; but what about our duty to keep our character and to preserve the achievements that only Western societies have managed? This, at least, is what Donnelly is calling upon us to recognise.

Donnelly claims to be optimistic that the tide is turning with 70 per cent plus not wanting to change the date of Australia Day; and 88 per cent of people over 50 telling one survey that modern Australia is "too politically correct" and 74 per cent that "political correctness annoyed them". Things are about to change, he says, when someone as in tune with the zeitgeist as the tennis great Martina Navratilova takes issue with the right of any man who merely self-identifies as female to compete in women's sport.

I hope Kevin's right; but suspect that the accusation of being "deeply transphobic" will unsettle Navratilova, as it has silenced so many people who might otherwise have spoken out in defence of what's only lately become politically incorrect. For all those that have had enough of the crime of political correctness, this is your book and your way to fight back because if the silent majority stays silent, it will no longer be the majority.

Peta Credlin, Sky News commentator and journalist.

A Politically Correct Dictionary and Guide

*Language is power,
life and the instrument of culture,
the instrument of domination and of liberation.*
Angela Carter

INTRODUCTION

There's no doubt political correctness is controlling how we speak and interact with others both at work and in our private lives. Political correctness even controls how we think, how public issues are decided and how politicians, policy makers and the media (with a few exceptions) frame the national debate and decide contentious issues.

While we all agree there is no place for personal abuse, unfair discrimination or deciding the merits of a case based on prejudice and bias, the political correctness movement is more than just about being civil, treating all with respect and basing one's beliefs and arguments on logic and reason.

Political correctness is a form of groupthink and language control used by the cultural-left to enforce its ideology on individuals and society more broadly. An ideology and form of thought control that can be traced to the Marxist concept of 'critical theory' and the belief that the way to radically change society is to engage in the battle of hearts and minds and to take the long march through the institutions.

Drawing on the Frankfurt School in Germany during the 1920s and the works of the Italian Marxist Antonio Gramsci the belief is the most effective way for the cultural-left to gain control is to infiltrate and dominate institutions such as the family, schools and universities, the media, government, the church and intermediary organisations including professional associations and unions.

While initially drawing on critical theory involving a Marxist critique of society political correctness has subsequently morphed into a rainbow alliance of theories, including: neo-Marxism, deconstructionism, postmodernism, second and third wave feminism and gender, sexuality and post-colonial theories.

As a result with issues as diverse as multiculturalism, the environment and sustainability, gender and sexuality, immigration, race relations, religion, the nature and significance of Western civilisation and the role of government, the debate is framed in terms of what is politically correct and what is not.

And instead of such issues being properly debated and discussed, those who refuse to conform are personally attacked as out of touch, conservative and backward looking. Criticise multiculturalism or immigration and you are racist, xenophobic and a white supremacist. Suggest that it's normal for children to be either boys and girls and that the love between a woman and a man should be celebrated and you are homophobic, transphobic and guilty of heteronormativity. Defend Christianity and you are a god-botherer and a paedophile; and defend Western civilisation, you are labelled as Eurocentric and guilty of whiteness and oppressing so-called victim groups.

Whether flamed and vilified on social networking sites, attacked in the print and electronic media, socially ostracised or in fear of not being promoted or losing your job, the reality is that political correctness represents a clear and present danger. Even worse, instead of being able to discuss issues in a rational and impartial way, debate is shut down and reduced to *ad hominem* attacks based on emotion and politically correct groupthink.

Although drawing on the Frankfurt School and Gramsci, the political correctness movement was given renewed impetus and became even more dominant as a result of the 1960s 'cultural revolution'. A time when students from the Sorbonne took to the streets in Paris, the Vietnam moratorium movement was at its height, the rights of minorities and identity politics took centre stage and cultural-left academics took control of university faculties and the school curriculum. As noted by the Australian academic Alan Barcan in *Sociological Theory and Educational Reality*:

> *The essential feature of the cultural revolution of 1967 – 1974 was the rejection of traditional authority. The most startling aspect of this was the new sexual freedom. The new morality favoured relativism; absolute beliefs, based on Christianity or liberal humanism, became unfashionable. Politically, a new radicalism and a new concern for minorities emerged.*

As a result political correctness is stifling debate, destroying the English language and imposing a distorted ideology that is undermining our institutions and our way of life. Best illustrated by George Orwell's 1984, where free expression and open debate are replaced by Big Brother and Newspeak, anyone who disagrees or thinks independently is guilty of 'thoughtcrime' and suffers as a result.

In the following dictionary and guide I detail examples of politically correct and incorrect language that dominate and influence how we communicate and think. As Orwell knew so well the ability to conceptualise and think independently and rationally depends on the ability to use language without interference. Once words are corrupted and used as vehicles to indoctrinate and coerce then the freedom and liberties we too easily take for granted are lost.

It should not surprise that one of the first acts of a dictatorship whether 'left' or 'right' is to take control of the media, universities and schools and to ensure the language people use and how issues are conceptualised and discussed reinforces its oppressive and destructive political agenda and world view.

Australian examples include government departments and corporations like Qantas arguing descriptions like 'mum and dad' and pronouns like 'she and he', 'him and her' are no longer acceptable as they might offend LGBTIQ+ people. Even the peak professional body responsible for advising English teachers has fallen victim; in an editorial published in *English in Australia* discussing the need to emphasise LGBTIQ+ issues in the classroom the statement is made "Their, they and them are used as alternatives to gendered pronouns".

Political correctness has also led to the creation of a host of new words and expressions that arise almost every week and, if not employed, have the power to condemn one as politically incorrect and not being 'Woke'. Short people are renamed as 'vertically challenged', manholes as 'personnel access structures' and old people become 'chronologically challenged'. To be guilty of 'bierasure' is to deny or ignore the existence and importance of bi-sexuality, 'Cissexism' is the mistaken belief that all people are heterosexual and 'whiteness' is a description used to criticise a curriculum that privileges what is condemned as a Eurocentric, oppressive and supremacist Western view of culture and history.

The second half of the book gives readers a better understanding of the origins and nature of political correctness. To paraphrase John Maynard Keynes, 'those who believe themselves to be quite exempt from any intellectual influence are usually the slaves of some defunct theorist'. Those advocating today's alliance of radical cultural-left theories whether they know it or not are the products of past ideologies and political philosophies.

As already mentioned, Marxism and the Frankfurt School as well as Antonio Gramsci are primarily responsible for the rise of critical theory and political correctness. More recently cultural-left academics including Michael Foucault, Louis Althusser, Pierre Bourdieu, Jacques Derrida, Simone De Beauvoir, Julia Kristeva have had a significant influence. While often in disagreement, such academics are responsible for formulating the ideas and strategies that underpin political correctness and that explain how and why it has been so successful in dominating public discourse, social policy, politics and university and school education.

Such is the impact of political correctness that in universities and schools knowledge is no longer considered inherently worthwhile or impartial. Knowledge is defined as a socio-cultural construct that enforces the power of ruling elites and is used to subjugate and oppress disadvantaged groups such as the working class, women, LGBTIQ+ people and those who are not white nor European.

While there is no doubt the history of Western civilisation, similar to other civilisations, involves exploitation, cruelty and violence and it is wrong to hide the sins of the past cultural-left academics are always negative and unrelenting in their attacks. Academics opposed to establishing centres to teach Western civilisation, funded by the Ramsay bequest, argue the history of Europe, the United Kingdom, Australia and the Western world in general is one solely of greed, exploitation, oppression and violence.

In English faculties literary classics like *Othello, Great Expectations, Pride and Prejudice, Huckleberry Finn, Heart of Darkness* and *Moby Dick* are deconstructed in terms of power relationships involving the new trinity of 'gender, ethnicity and class'. Children's stories like *Little Black Sambo, The Far Away Tree* and *Thomas the Tank Engine* have also fallen victim to the political correctness movement.

In the Australian national curriculum made compulsory for all schools, government and non-government, political correctness dominates. Across all year levels from preparatory to year 10 teachers are required to incorporate indigenous, Asian and sustainability content and perspectives while Western civilisation, especially Judeo-Christianity and liberalism as a political philosophy, receive scant attention.

How teachers teach and interact with students and what happens in the classroom are also dominated by critical theory and political correctness. Instead of explicit teaching, setting high expectations and passing and failing students teachers are described as facilitators, all students are winners and, as a result, Australian classrooms are among the worst in the OECD for disruptive and badly behaved students. The purpose of education, instead of educating in a balanced and impartial way, is to deconstruct and critique society and to enact the cultural-left's utopian alternative.

Programs like Safe Schools promote radical gender and sexuality theories where primary school children are told they have the freedom to self-identify as whatever gender they are most comfortable with. In relation to being transgender the 'Gender Questioning' booklet tells students there "are no limitations on what your gender and identity can be". For those students wanting to undergo a gender transition process another booklet tells teachers "It may be possible to consider a student a mature minor and able to make decisions without parental consent".

For those students who have undergone gender transition, with or without parental consent, the booklet titled 'Guide to supporting a student to affirm or transition gender identity at school' argues that sporting activities should not be segregated "on the basis of sex or gender identity". Schools are also told they should permit transgender students to use the "toilets, changing rooms, showers and swimming facilities based on the student's gender identity and the facilities they will feel most comfortable with".

While there is no doubt that political correctness has corrupted society and undermined the liberty and freedom we take for granted and continues to do so, there is cause for optimism. Australians are generally levelheaded, practical and sane and such is the extreme nature of political correctness that many are now saying enough is enough. Common sense and the realisation that there is so much to acknowledge and celebrate outweigh the dark and depressing influence of identity politics, victimhood and the incessant complaint that Western societies are riven with inequality and disadvantage.

The fact that 70% of those interviewed do not want the date of Australia Day changed despite the cultural-left's cry of invasion day and genocide is one cause for optimism. A survey of older Australians recently carried out also illustrates that things are not as bleak as might appear. Of the 1,000 people aged over 50 surveyed 88 per cent thought people in modern Australia were too politically correct, 74 per cent said people who strived to be politically correct annoyed them and 45 per cent said they tried to avoid being politically correct just for the sake of it.

In a recently completed survey carried out by the Australian Broadcasting Commission, 68% of those surveyed agreed political correctness had gone too far. Not surprisingly, given the consensus that the Australian Labor Party fails to properly represent its working class, blue-collar base, 52% of those identifying as Labor voters also expressed concerns about the negative impact of PC.

The activities and effectiveness of think-tanks like the Perth based Mannkal Economic Foundation, Sydney's the Centre for Independent Studies, Melbourne's Institute of Public Affairs and Hobart's Christopher Dawson Centre for Cultural Studies also suggest the pendulum is moving to what can be described as the sensible centre. Tertiary institutions like Campion College and the work of the Ramsay Centre for Western Civilisation also demonstrate that political correctness is not all pervasive and powerful.

The election of Donald Trump by what Hilary Clinton terms a "basket of deplorables", the decision by the British people to support Brexit, the rise of centre-right anti-immigration parties in Europe, the demonstrations in France by Yellow Vest protesters, while unnecessarily violent, provide further evidence that more and more people are ready and willing to react against cultural-left ideology and elites and to assert their sanity and independence. Scott Morrison's unexpected and dramatic win at the 2019 federal election as a result of appealing to the quiet Australians also suggests there is cause for optimism.

POLITICALLY CORRECT AND INCORRECT WORDS AND EXPRESSIONS

*But if thought corrupts language,
language can also corrupt thought.*
George Orwell, *1984*.

1. **Ableism.** An unwarranted and unjustified prejudice against those who are disabled committed by able bodied people.

2. **Aboriginal and Torres Strait Islander science.** The Australian Curriculum Assessment and Reporting Authority (ACARA) argues indigenous science must be taught at all year levels in science classes. The justification for putting indigenous science on the same footing as Western science is because teachers need to "provide a more culturally responsive curriculum". Schools are also told "It is crucial that our curriculum effectively includes respect and understanding of 65,000+ years of Aboriginal and Torres Strait Islander history".

   Schools are told that "Indigenous history, culture, knowledge and understanding can be incorporated into teaching core scientific concepts" and that Australia's indigenous peoples "have explored the many wonders of our continent for millennia" and "through their rich enduring legacy, we can inspire the same instinct to explore in our students today". Critics of putting indigenous science on the same footing as Western science are described as promoting a "racist diatribe" that ignores that indigenous peoples "lived here before 'Western enlightenment' arrived and started raping and killing them". The Aboriginal activist Warren Mundine, while accepting the need to teach about indigenous history and culture, argues differently when saying science is science regardless of ethnicity or race. He argues "What is indigenous physics? Physics is physics. If we are to compete in the job market we must learn technology and engineering, we need to be taught subjects properly".

3. **Ageism.** The belief that those old enough to remember black and white TVs, red telephone boxes, garage pump attendants and Xerox machines are obsolete and of little value. The Sydney academic Teena Clerke was a victim of ageism when a student complained on an online survey seeking feedback from students "This woman is so old her views are redundant. She hasn't designed anything since the internet. Why do we need her?". Older people, otherwise known as the chronologically challenged, are digitally inept and adhere to obsolete behaviour including civility, good manners, not eating in public and expecting children to be well behaved and respect adults.

4. **Agitprop.** The Oxford Dictionary defines agitprop as "political (originally communist) propaganda, especially in art or literature". The expression is used more widely now to refer to any attempt, usually by the cultural-left, to use the media to circulate propaganda and fake news to influence social and political debates. President Trump regularly criticises the American liberal-left media for being guilty of fake news and after a meeting with President Putin tweeted "The Summit with Russia was a great success, except with the real

enemy of the people, the Fake News Media".

5. **Alcoholic.** Describing somebody as an alcoholic is demeaning and offensive as such individuals are often the victims of events beyond their control. More politically correct alternatives include 'substance abuse survivor' and 'chemically inconvenienced individual'.

6. **Alt-right.** Short for alternative right and the expression is used to describe extreme right wing organisations and individuals who reject conservatism as not going far enough and instead espouse a racist, offensive ideology that sometimes borders on violence.

7. **Anchor baby.** A term originating in America used to describe babies born to illegal immigrants that enable the parents to have a better chance of claiming citizenship and being allowed to resettle. After the Australian Home Affairs Minister Peter Dutton used the expression he was attacked in the twittersphere by Noel Miller as follows: "Anchor baby is a racist term used in the US by anti-immigration activists, demonising children of non-citizen adults, who allegedly use their kids who were born in the US to gain citizenship".

8. **Andorcentrism.** Defined as privileging men by treating them as dominant and excluding women and LGBTIQ+ people. For example, the expression 'he's a man's man' is phallocentric as it suggests that manliness in boys and men is an admirable quality, when second

and third wave feminists argue they should be more like women. The politically correct alternative to 'he's a man's man' is 'zie is a non-gendered individual's intersex person who should be celebrated in a non-binary way'.

9. **Animals.** Otherwise known as 'non-human sentient creatures' as the description 'animals' suggests an inferior status leading to exploitation and cruelty. 'The Journal of Animal Ethics', edited by Reverend Professor Andrew Linzey, argues 'wild animals' is unacceptable as it suggests an uncivilised, unrestrained and barbarous existence.

10. **Australia Day.** Aboriginal activists argue Australia Day is a "day of mourning and a day of shame" and describe the arrival of the First Fleet as an invasion. An invasion, according to Dr Hannah McGlade a Senior Indigenous Research Fellow at Curtin University, that led to the "genocide" of Australia's indigenous people. Those celebrating the arrival of the First Fleet and the establishment of a British penal colony are condemned as Eurocentric and guilty of white supremacism.

11. **Bald.** A description once used to describe those, usually men, with no hair. Politically correct alternatives include 'follicularly challenged' and 'hair disadvantaged'.

12. **BAME.** A politically correct acronym referring to those living in the UK who are black, Asian, minority ethnic. Used on the basis that descriptions such as English or

British reinforce white privilege and deny the identity of those who are categorised and mis-treated as the 'Other'.

13. **BC/AD.** Traditional Christian terms once used to describe the period before and after the birth of Christ with BC referring to the period before the birth of Christ and AD coming from the Latin Anno Domini referring to "in the year of the Lord". Such terms privilege Christianity as a religion and are offensive in our diverse, multi-faith, multicultural society; a society that celebrates diversity and difference and where all cultures and religions are equal. The politically correct alternatives are BCE (Before the Common Era) and CE (Common Era).

14. **Bed wetters.** Originating in America the expression is used in Australia to describe those centre-left parliamentary members of the centre-right Liberal Party who betrayed the then Prime Minister Tony Abbott by replacing him with Malcolm Turnbull. They argued Abbott was too conservative and that as Turnbull was seen as progressive in areas like climate change, same-sex marriage and multiculturalism he would be more electorally appealing. In the 2016 Commonwealth election the Turnbull government was nearly defeated and such were Turnbull's failures and inability to lead that he was replaced as Prime Minister by Scott Morrison in 2018.

15. **Bierasure.** The 'Monash University Diversity and Inclusion Glossary' defines bierasure as "questioning or denying the existence or legitimacy of bisexuality (either in general or in regard to an individual)".

16. **Binary.** Binary concepts like male/female, heterosexual/homosexual, civilised/primitive, black/white are politically incorrect as they reinforce and reproduce an inequitable system of exploitation and marginalisation associated with Western, capitalist power structures. For example, to describe pre-1788 Aboriginal tribes as primitive because they had not invented the wheel and there were no printing presses, roads, buildings, steam engines or clearly defined and sophisticated forms of law and government is to be guilty of imposing a Eurocentric concept employed to justify the invasion. The binary description male/female is also offensive as it reinforces the belief that just because approximately 98% of Australians self-identify as women and men that heterosexuality is the norm.

17. **Biological essentialism.** Research proving that many of the differences between men and women are determined by nature, as girls at birth have XX chromosomes while boys have XY, is described by radical feminists as 'biological determinism' imposed by a patriarchal, oppressive society. Second and third wave feminists prefer to believe that gender and sexuality are social constructs as then all they have to do in order to change society is to mandate people's

beliefs and attitudes and all will be well.

18. **BirthStrike.** Blythe Pepino, a British musician and climate activist, founded the movement BirthStrike after reaching the conclusion it was unfair to have children given government inaction and the existential threat represented by climate change. In a report in The Guardian (March, 2019) Pepino warns of "climate breakdown and civilisation collapse" and what she terms "the severity of an ecological crisis" caused by global warming. In an interview with *Elle* magazine the American singer and actress Miley Cyrus also warns of the end of the world and the decision not to have children. After comparing how humans exploit the earth with how women are exploited Cyrus states "We just take and take and expect it to keep producing... And it's exhausted. It can't produce. We're getting handed a piece-of-shit planet, and I refuse to hand that down to my child".

19. **Blacking up/Black facing.** An example of cultural appropriation where white people blacken their faces. While common on screen and stage in the past blacking up is now considered demeaning and offensive to people of colour. An example of blacking up includes the 1964 film Mary Poppins when she appears on the roof with her face covered in soot and dancing with chimney sweeps. The characters are described as "Hottentots" and in the New York Times Daniel Pollack-Pelzer argues "These aren't really black Africans; they're

grinning white dancers in blackface. It's a parody of black menace; it's even posted on a white nationalist website as evidence of the film's racial hierarchy".

20. **Blacktivist.** Refers to those advocating the rights of Aboriginal and Torres Strait Islander people against a government that is considered Eurocentric, oppressive and responsible for the genocide, dispossession and theft that has occurred since the arrival of the First Fleet. The fact that indigenous Australians have the same political and legal rights as all the other Australians, that decisions like Mabo guarantee indigenous ownership of land and that billions are spent every year to support the Aborigine and Torres Strait Islander industry is ignored.

21. **Blind leading the blind.** Visually impaired people consider this expression offensive as it mistakenly suggests their condition denotes a weakness or inability to see things clearly. The correct expression is 'the sight impaired leading the visually challenged'.

22. **Body shaming.** Defined as abusing and shaming people whose body shapes do not conform to the white, patriarchal, capitalist, marketing stereotype. When the British TV personality Jameela Jamil was confronted by a man commenting about her appearance she answered "Never walk up to someone and tell them how much better they could look. You're not being nice, you're shaming them for the way they currently look. You're

also being extremely weird".

23. **Brown facing.** Similar to black facing this involves a white person being guilty of masquerading as a person of colour. One of the most high profile examples of brown facing involves the Canadian Prime Minister Pierre Trudeau who when teaching at a private school attended an Arabian Night's function with a brown face. On being publicly outed Trudeau, who has a reputation as politically correct and Woke, admitted to reporters "I'm pissed off with myself. I'm disappointed with myself".

24. **Captain Cook.** Captain Cook is a DWEM (dead, white, European male). By claiming what is now the east coast of Australia for Britain in 1770 Cook shares responsibility for the white invasion and the 'genocide' of Australia's indigenous peoples. In fact there was no genocide. Most Aborigines who died were victims of new diseases.

Stan Grant, a commentator on the ABC, when discussing Cook's statue in Sydney's Hyde Park argues "Yet this statue speaks to emptiness, it speaks to our invisibility; it says that nothing truly mattered, nothing truly counted until a white sailor first walked on these shores. The statue speaks still to *terra nullius* and the violent rupture of Aboriginal society and a legacy of pain and suffering that endures today".

25. **Change adaptors.** According to a report in *The Age* (March 26, 2019) the principal of Melbourne's Siena College argues librarians are obsolete. Siena College now has what are described as change adaptors who "host discussions with students and teach 'soft skills' such as ethical and creative thinking". The principal also argues "If you think about it you don't need to go to the library to do research and you don't need a librarian to talk to you about interesting literature or books".

26. **Christopher Columbus.** Like Captain Cook, Columbus who discovered America, is now decidedly politically incorrect and considered yet another DWEM. Los Angeles has replaced Columbus Day with Indigenous Day as contemporary America is built on the exploitation and enslavement of indigenous inhabitants who lived in harmony with the land and coexisted peacefully. Before Europeans invaded what is now America the tribes that existed never engaged in warfare, stole from one another or exploited one another's territories.

27. **Christianity.** Defined as a Eurocentric, oppressive myth based on superstition and a mistaken belief in miracles and the afterlife. The father of communism Karl Marx describes religion as "the opium of the people" and the English academic Richard Dawkins in *The God Delusion* argues "Faith can be very, very dangerous, and deliberately to implant it into the vulnerable mind of an innocent child is a grievous wrong."

28. **Christianophobia.** Patrick Sookhdeo in *The Death of Western Christianity* argues we are living in an intolerant and oppressive "anti-Christian age". He describes Christianophobia as "a state of fear and hatred against Christianity and Christians".

29. **Christmas carols.** Used by religious adherents to indoctrinate young children with binary concepts like right and wrong, good and bad and treating others as you would have them treat you. Many schools ban Christmas carols as they privilege Christianity over other religions and faiths in Australia's multicultural, multi-faith society. In order to celebrate diversity and difference if carols are sung, they must not refer to the birth of Christ or celebrate Christmas as a religious occasion.

30. **Chronologically challenged.** Otherwise known as the aged or old people (see Ageism).

31. **Cisgender.** Refers to those Cismen and Ciswomen who have been conditioned to be happy with the biological sex they were assigned at birth. The blogger Jeff Estevez argues that Cisgender is a capitalist inspired, oppressive concept employed to erase the fact that there are multiple genders, he argues "Colonialism and other power structures have tried really hard to erase this and enforce a strict gender binary so that there is also a strict power hierarchy".

32. **Cisnormativity.** The Monash University's 'Inclusive Teaching Toolkit' describes this as assuming "that everyone is cisgender and that all people will continue to identify with the gender they were assigned at birth". Cisnormativity erases the existence of trans, queer and gender diverse people.

33. **Cissexism.** The Safe Schools 'OMG I'm Trans' booklet describes Cissexim as "The assumption that everyone is straight and Cisgender".

34. **Citizenship.** Being a citizen no longer involves owing allegiance to the country where you were born or that has granted you citizenship. Instead, as detailed in the national Civics and Citizenship curriculum "Citizenship means different things to people at different times and depending on personal perspectives, their social situation and where they live". Citizenship involves multiple perspectives that "reflect personal, social, spatial and temporal dimensions of citizenship". As such it is wrong to deny citizenship to those Muslim Australians like Neil Prakash who fought with ISIS in the Middle East to establish an Islamic caliphate.

35. **Clickbait.** A text or link that tempts the user to click on the link and go to the associated site on the internet.

36. **Climate denier.** Even though the science is far from settled regarding man-made global warming, politically correct activists denounce any who disagree

with the prevailing orthodoxy as climate deniers. Bjorn Lomborg who questions the causal relationship between carbon and global warming is attacked in the Twittersphere as "an idiotic moron" and someone dedicated to promoting a "neo-conservative conspiracy agenda".

37. **Cognitive dissonance.** Refers to the ability to hold two or more contradictory thoughts or beliefs at the one time and not to understand they are in opposition. Described by George Orwell as 'Doublethink' involving the "power of holding two contradictory beliefs in one's mind simultaneously and accepting both of them". An example of cognitive dissonance is when feminists fail to criticise Islamic states like Saudi Arabia for oppressing women even though they are committed to equal rights for both sexes. The fact that Islamic fundamentalism disadvantages women is ignored on the basis we must celebrate diversity and difference (the new code for multiculturalism) because all cultures are equal.

38. **Competition.** Competing against others and being ranked in terms of performance breeds inequality, reinforces disadvantage and favours the wealthy. The Australian Education Union argues "Reliance on competition is a primary cause of inequalities of educational outcomes because students from certain social groups are advantaged by competitive selection methods. Competitive selection also sets students against each other rather than encouraging co-

operative learning methods" (AEU '1998 Curriculum Policy'). A teacher union official from Western Australia argues "The union was philosophically opposed to grades because they were educationally unsound and could brand students as failures from a young age". Far preferable, according to this care, share, grow philosophy, is to postpone failure until students have grown up and have to compete in the real world.

Andrew Hamilton on the Eureka website condemns competition as it "makes strangers out of friends (and causes) fear and envy to dominate love, the desire to possess, to master the desire to give, and individual desires to trump common needs, and reduces public conversation to conflict between interest groups with the rewards going to the most powerful. In a word, a world enslaved by competition is uncivilized".

39. **Compulsory heterosexuality.** Defined by the encyclopedia of glbtq culture as "the assumption that women and men are innately attracted to each other emotionally and sexually and that heterosexuality is normal and universal… in our society this leads to an institutionalized inequality of power". After referring to the writings of Adrienne Rich the dictionary states that this binary concept "is an institution designed to perpetuate male social and economic privilege".

40. **Constructivism.** The Australian Commonwealth's report 'Teaching Reading' defines constructivism as "a theory of learning that builds on the work of Piaget, Bruner and Vygotsky, which views students as inherently active, self-regulating learners who construct knowledge cooperatively with other learners in developmentally appropriate ways... Adoption of a constructivist approach in the classroom involves a shift from predominantly teacher-directed methods to student-centred, active discovery learning and immersion approaches via cooperative group work, discussion focused on investigations and problem solving".

Constructivism can also be traced back to the American educator John Dewey and the French philosopher Jean-Jacques Rousseau – both who argue that learning should be natural, centred on the world of the child and where the teacher is seen as a 'facilitator' and 'guide by the side'. The NSW academic John Sweller argues that even though this progressive approach to learning has dominated Australian and American education since the late 60s it is ineffective and responsible for falling standards. Sweller argues in favour of explicit teaching where students are expected to master what is essential until it can be re-called automatically.

41. **Cooking with gas.** An obsolete expression before people were 'Woke' as they still believed gas provided an effective and beneficial method of heating and cooking.

42. **Cow's milk.** The activist group People for the Ethical Treatment of Animals (PETA) argues cow's milk should not be consumed as "dairy milk has long been a symbol of white supremacy". The group's website argues "Rape is perhaps the single most heinous crime involving both power and violence. But it's standard procedure in the dairy industry. Like all mammals, cows produce milk only during and after pregnancy, so roughly every nine months, cows on dairy farms are forcibly impregnated so that their milk production will continue. They're restrained on what the farmers themselves call 'rape racks' while insemination instruments are shoved into their vaginas".

43. **Critical theory.** Originating in the Frankfurt School in Germany during the 1920s critical theory involves evaluating and critiquing capitalism to unmask how those in control oppress and marginalise the disadvantaged and the dispossessed. The Marxist academics involved realised the communist revolution was never going to occur in the West through violence and that the focus had to shift from economic issues to the battle of ideas and the long march through the institutions like universities and schools, the church, family and the media. As argued by Wanda Skowronska in a paper titled '1960s psychologists: beguiling ideologues and smiling assassins': "Critical theory did not aim to tear down the economic base of western society as, with the force of history, it was inevitably going to collapse anyway. It aimed rather at tearing

down the cultural superstructure which supposedly reflected the powerful controllers of the economic system and this would enable the collapse of western civilisation".

Critical theory now involves a rainbow alliance of theories including: neo-Marxism, postmodernism, deconstructionism and feminist, gender, queer and post-colonial theories. Even though Western civilisation is responsible for record levels of prosperity, health, stability and freedom as well as miraculous advances in medicine, science and technology it is considered inherently sexist, heteronormative, exploitive, Eurocentric and guilty of reinforcing inequality and disadvantage.

44. **Critical literacy.** On offshoot of critical theory, critical literacy is an approach to English teaching based on the work of the South American Marxist educator Paulo Freire. His books *Pedagogy of the Oppressed* and *Education: The Practice of Freedom* have had a profound effect on how reading is taught and how literature is analysed and evaluated. Central to Freire's work is the belief that education should be empowering and liberating and directed at challenging the status quo and changing capitalist society.

Freire argues the true purpose of education is to allow students "to perceive themselves in dialectical relationship with their social reality (and) to assume an increasingly critical attitude toward the world and so to transform it". Practices like rote learning, teachers as experts and failing to address real-life issues are criticised as promoting a "banking concept" where learners, supposedly, are passive and treated as empty vessels waiting to be filled with knowledge. The Australian Association for the Teaching of English and the Australian Curriculum Studies Association are strong advocates of critical literacy and argue that English as a subject must be a vehicle to deconstruct texts in terms of power relationships and to empower so-called victim groups; including women, LGBTIQ+ people, people of colour, migrants and the working class.

45. **Cultural appropriation.** The Australian HuffPost defines this as "the act of taking or using things from a culture that is not your own, especially without showing that you understand or respect this culture". Examples include a Perth mother making the mistake of allowing her white, privileged son to dress as his hero, the AFL footballer of colour Nic Naitanui, for a school dress up day. For this the mother was condemned and her son expelled from the party for disrespecting the 'Other'.

Hollywood is especially susceptible to claims of cultural appropriation witnessed by Scarlet Johansson being made to withdraw from playing the role of a transgender character. On Twitter Elise Bauman criticized Johansson arguing "the way you can use your privilege as a white Ciswoman is to amplify the voices of underrepresented communities, not speak for them". The famous Shakespearean actor Sir Lawrence Olivier is guilty of cultural appropriation as one of his most famous roles is playing the person of colour Othello. Another example of cultural appropriation is Peter Sellers playing the role of an accident prone Indian in the Hollywood movie The Party.

46. **Cultural Marxism.** Whereas classical Marxism focuses on overthrowing capitalism by taking control of the modes and means of production cultural Marxism emphasises transforming society by engaging in the culture wars. (See also 'Critical theory', 'Culture wars' and the 'Frankfurt School'.)

47. **Culture Wars.** The English conservative politician Michael Gove in *Celcius 7/7* refers to the German-based Frankfurt School and the rise of the New Left during the mid-to-late 1960s when detailing the origins of the culture wars. Gove suggests the focus of radical change shifted from economic issues to social and cultural. The Australian Prime Minister John Howard also argues that one of the key battlegrounds between conservatives and the cultural-left involves the battle of ideas; illustrated by conflicting interpretations of Australian history and the significance of Western civilisation.

48. **Dead naming.** This involves referring to the previous gender of a person who has undergone transition from male to female or female to male. The American

Wikileaks whistle blower Chelsea Manning, the American soldier convicted of treason for leaking secret documents, after undergoing transition to a woman, refuses to be addressed according to her previous gender. As reported by the ABC on being interviewed by Peter Greste who referred to Manning's pre-transition gender identity Manning interrupted Greste saying "please don't deadname me". Given the rise of cultural-left inspired anti-discrimination legislation the fear is that dead naming might soon be a punishable offence.

49. **Deaf as a post.** Considered offensive to those who are hearing impaired as it suggests they have the same hearing qualities as a wooden post.

50. **Deconstruction.** Often attributed to the French academic Jacques Derrida deconstruction, in the words of the Cambridge Dictionary, involves analysing "a text in order to show there is no fixed meaning but that it can be understood in a different way by each reader". The meaning of a text varies from person to person as the encounter is subjective; there is no authorial intention as the author is non-existent (as in dead) and words have no inherent meaning as they are simply 'signifiers' that mean different things to different people.

51. **Degenderize.** Refers to expunging heteronormative gender specific pronouns and descriptions. The City of Berkeley in California revised its municipal code in 2019 to "replace all instances of gendered pronouns with the

singular 'they'... and to indicate that whenever a gender-neutral pronoun is used, it shall be deemed to include the feminine and the masculine also". The city officials argue "broadening social awareness of transgender and gender nonconforming identities has brought to light the importance of non-binary gender inclusivity".

52. **Denier.** A description used by cultural-left activists to condemn and silence anyone who questions or contradicts politically correct orthodoxy in relation to issues such as: man-made global warming, multiculturalism, gender and sexuality and feminism. As in "everyone knows the science is proven when it comes to man-made global warming and those who disagree like the scientists associated with the UK based Global Warming Policy Foundation are wrong; they are climate deniers".

53. **Digital natives.** School children are no longer described as students with the expectation they be taught by teachers (otherwise known as 'guides by the side' or 'facilitators'). As a result of the digital revolution the printed word is obsolete as millennials have been surrounded by computers, mobile phones, laptops, social networking sites and screens since birth. Old fashioned learning and knowledge is outdated as students are now 'knowledge navigators' where searching the web offers unlimited information and possibilities for exploration. Digital natives through a process of collaborative, negotiated goal setting and

inquiry-based, self-directed learning are free to explore the world-wide web making teachers redundant.

Ignored is the research carried out by the Organisation for Economic Co-operation and Development concluding an over reliance on the new technologies is counter-productive as standards suffer and students under-perform as measured by international tests such as PISA.

54. **Disability shaming.** Abusing or making fun of those who are disabled (see Ableism).

55. **Dissing.** Originally associated with the American hip hop scene dissing involves showing disrespect and insulting someone. As in "you are so fat you must have shares in McDonalds" – "Hey, don't diss and fat shame me".

56. **Disprivileged.** Involves identifying as a victim group that is oppressed and disadvantaged by mainstream capitalist, white, Eurocentric, queerphobic, misogynist society. Juliet Moses in the Australian edition of 'The Spectator' details a privilege worksheet given to students at an American high school in which they add or sub-track points according to their religion, ethnicity, skin colour, sexuality and gender. Those who are white, Christian, male and able bodied score highest as they are privileged. If you are black, gay, Muslim, a woman or genderqueer you score minus points thus

proving you are disprivileged as Western, capitalist and Eurocentric societies like America marginalise and disempower those who are not mainstream.

57. **Diversity Toolkits.** An example of a Diversity Toolkit is the Flinders University's 'Cultural Diversity and Inclusive Practice (CDIP) Toolkit'. The purpose of the toolkit is "to sustain and enhance a culturally inclusive environment at Flinders University. Cultural diversity refers to the similarities and differences among cultures across ethnic, religious and language boundaries, for example". Whereas universities once prioritised the search for knowledge, wisdom and truth based on Western concepts of reason and rationality the focus is now on diversity, difference, identity politics and victimhood. The Toolkit defines students in terms of their "national, racial, ethnic, religious and language origins" instead of what they hold in common as university students pursuing tertiary studies (see also trigger warnings and Safe Space).

58. **Doxing.** Involves gathering personal information and data about individuals, usually from social networking sites, and making it public on the internet without their knowledge or permission. Doxing is often used to shame, vilify and attack individuals and groups and has the power to go viral in a short time and is difficult, if not impossible, to counter.

59. **Dunny man.** A now obsolete term considered offensive as demeaning and phallocentric; the preferred alternative is 'a non-gendered, sanitation person' or 'non-binary hygiene worker'.

60. **DWEMs.** The 1992 American publication titled *The Official Politically Correct Dictionary & Handbook* defines DWEMs as "dead, white, European males" responsible for the evils and sins committed by Western civilisation. As argued by the 150 Sydney University academics opposed to establishing a Western Civilisation Centre funded by the Ramsay bequest, teaching about Western civilisation promotes "European supremacism" and a "conservative, culturally essentialist and Eurocentric vision". Academics at the University of Queensland are also opposed to establishing a centre funded by the Ramsay bequest on the basis it is an example of "cultural chauvinism" and "whitewashing or colonialism".

61. **Easter worshippers.** After Christian churches in Sri Lanka were bombed and hundreds of Christians killed while celebrating the death and ascension of Jesus President Obama and Hilary Clinton instead of acknowledging religion described the attack as one involving "Easter worshippers". Critics suggest this is yet another PC example of christianophobia.

62. **Ecofascism/ecofascist.** The Urban Dictionary defines ecofascism as someone "who advocates for

the subordination of individual self-interest to the ecofundamentalism of the Green lobby". In its most extreme form ecofascism relies on threats, intimidation and violence to achieve its ultimate gaol of ridding personkind's destructive impact on nature. An example of ecofascism is the Aussie Farms website making public the locations of homes and farms of primary producers across Australia and inciting protestors to invade properties involved in animal husbandry.

63. **Emotional labour.** Gemma Hartley in a piece published in 'Harper's Bazaar' uses the expression to describe the added burden women face at home. Hartley argues as well as physical labour such women are responsible for emotional labour; she writes "It's so exhausting and frustrating to be the manager of the household and the manager of everyone's emotional state". As noted by Mary Ward in *The Age,* the term is now used "as a catch-all for gendered labour inequality, particularly in domestic partnerships". Dr Hannah McCann from Melbourne University extends the definition further by describing it as "shorthand for any work that women do that is ephemeral and not explicitly valued".

64. **Equality of outcomes.** In opposition to equality of opportunity (where all are given the same opportunity to succeed based on merit and ability) equality of outcomes involves positive discrimination and affirmative action for victim groups. Imposing quotas to mandate the percentage of women in parliament

or the percentage of women on company boards is a policy based on achieving equality of outcomes. In the United States there is positive discrimination for people of colour for entry to colleges and universities (except of Asian students who for some reason achieve academic success based on ability and effort).

65. **Eurocentric.** As a result of post-colonial theory it is no longer acceptable to acknowledge or celebrate the achievements of those countries associated with the Europe and the United Kingdom. Instead of celebrating the grand narrative associated with Western civilisation that can be traced back to ancient Rome and Greece the West's legacy is oppressive and responsible for colonial exploitation and imperialism as well as climate change, the destruction of the world's ecosystem and the death of countless polar bears.

66. **Facilitators.** In the 21st century classroom teachers are described as facilitators as their expertise as teachers is no longer needed. Students, otherwise known as 'knowledge navigators' and 'digital natives', are involved in self-directed, inquiry based learning in an ever transient, digital, 21st century, global environment.

67. **Faith-phobia.** An extreme hatred and dislike of religious beliefs, especially Christianity, and the conviction there is no place for religion in public debates and government policy and decision-making. Even though parliaments across Australia begin with

the Lord's prayer and the Australian Constitution refers to "Almighty God" cultural-left critics argue Australia is a secular society and religious freedoms, in particular, must be curtailed. Except for Christian events like Christmas and Easter when secular critics enjoy their holidays and are happy to take advantage of family reunions, celebrations and time off work.

68. **False consciousness.** The Italian Marxist Antonio Gramsci argues that capitalist society is able to reproduce itself and maintain dominance and control by making unequal power relations appear acceptable and normal. As a result of false consciousness girls and boys might appear happy being Cisfemales and Cismales but this is only because society indoctrinates them with the belief that heterosexuality is preferable to being LGBTIQ+.

Girls who look forward to marriage, bearing children and being mothers and wives only do so because they live in a patriarchal society where what is expected and acceptable is determined by men to suit their selfish ends. Workers who are well paid, who achieve a high standard of living and lead a prosperous life, if only they were intelligent enough to realise, are being oppressed because of false consciousness. The reality is that they are disadvantaged and are being exploited by an inherently unjust and inequitable capitalist system.

69. **Fat shaming.** In 'You Have the Right to Remain Fat: A Manifesto' Virgie Tovar argues fat people are unfairly ostracised and made fun of because of fatness – otherwise known as being horizontally challenged. Tovar defines fatphobia as fat-shaming those who fail to conform to the 'ideal' body image imposed by a binary, heteronormative, capitalist, consumer driven society. The Commonwealth Minister for Sport, Bridget McKenzie, recently was accused of fat shaming when she mimicked having a bloated stomach while launching an Obesity campaign. She later apologised saying "I sincerely apologise for this very unfortunate photo taken as I demonstrated how my stomach felt after scrambled eggs reacted (with) yoghurt I had just eaten".

70. **Father Christmas.** A mythical figure created to dupe unsuspecting children with the belief if they are subservient and comply with the authoritarian demands of their parents they will be rewarded (See Santa Claus).

71. **Father's Day.** A phallocentric, binary ritual that privileges heterosexuality and the mistaken belief that children need to have a biological father. Alternative descriptions include 'A Non-binary, Gender Free Person's Day' and 'Parents and Carers Day'.

72. **Female.** An oppressive binary description of women that reinforces male dominance and the patriarchal

nature of capitalist, phallocentric society. The description also offends those self-identifying as non-gender, gender diverse, queer or in transition. A Monash University diversity guide warns against using the expression "female" as it is a "term that can be applied to animals and objects".

73. **Female colonisation.** Vania Phitidis on the HuffPost website argues as a result of false consciousness women fail to realise how they perceive themselves and self-identify is controlled by "patriarchy and capitalism". Women no longer control their bodies as they have been colonised by men only concerned with profit making and dominating women by enforcing a sexist, oppressive stereotype.

74. **Female assigned at birth.** Instead of being biologically determined and binary by nature sexuality and gender are 'assigned' on the basis that being a girl or a boy is a social construct imposed on innocent and unsuspecting babies by a heteronormative, transphobic society. What is 'assigned" can later be changed and some parents now refuse to name their baby at birth on the basis that it is too early to identify the child's gender.

75. **Feminism.** While there are various version of feminism (generally categorised as first, second and third wave) what all have in common is the belief that society is patriarchal and phallocentric where men dominate and

women lack equality. More extreme feminists argue men are inherently misogynist and violent towards women.

76. **Fillies.** A term used to describe female horses but politically incorrect when applied to women as sometimes happens in racing circles. Melissa Singer argues describing young ladies at the racetrack as fillies "reduces their participation in the sport to that of playthings and walking coat hangers and does little to advance gender equality". Singer also suggests that using descriptions like "sheilas, chicks, birds, girls, woozas, bitches" is also unacceptable as such labels "are often degrading, demeaning and, in worst cases, downright abusive".

77. **First Fleet.** Refers to the 11 ships and over 1480 men, women and children under the control of Admiral Arthur Phillip that arrived in what is now Sydney in 1788 to establish a British penal colony. While the event is officially celebrated on the 26th of January as the birth of modern day Australia critics describe it as an invasion leading to genocide (see Australia Day).

78. **First nations.** While nations is a Eurocentric concept employed to subjugate others and is foreign to the over 600 to 700 different indigenous tribes that existed when the First Fleet arrived in Botany Bay it has been appropriated by Aboriginal activists in their battle for constitutional recognition. As the expression 'First

nations' originated in Canada to describe its first inhabitants by employing the term Aboriginal activists are open to the charge of cultural appropriation.

79. **Flamed.** Refers to being personally attacked, vilified and abused in an online forum or via the internet and other digital media.

80. **Flight shaming.** Environmental activists argue that people should either restrict or stop flying as aeroplanes are increasingly contributing to global warming. The Swedish activist Bjorn Ferry suggests that those who fly unnecessarily are immoral and in Europe those who fly regularly are publicly shamed. An exception to flight shaming are the hundreds of government officials and environmental scientists and activists flying around the world on a regular basis to attend global warming events and conferences.

81. **Frankfurt School.** The Marxist inspired academics who established the Frankfurt School in Germany during the 1920s are responsible for developing critical theory – an approach to sociology, economics, history and philosophy that has led to a radical alliance of cultural-left theories, including: Neo-Marxism, extreme feminism, postmodernism, deconstructionism and gender, queer and post-colonial theories (See critical theory). As previously mentioned Michael Gove, the former UK Secretary of State for Education and in his book *Celsius 7/7*, argues "The thinkers of

the Frankfurt School revised Marxism as primarily a cultural rather than an economic movement. In place of anger at traditional capitalism, scorn was directed at the reigning values of the West".

82. **Fun police.** The American commentator Bill Maher criticises politically correct fun police for decreeing there be "no hula girls, no Indian chiefs, no Southern belles, no ninjas, gypsies" during Halloween. Maher goes on to argue "Not everything that merely alludes to another culture is racist, or cultural appropriation" and that "Halloween was always fun because it wasn't PC. Not being PC was almost the whole point of the holiday. But now everything has to turn into a federal case of snowflakes v. humor".

83. **Gaslighting.** Trans-activists describe gaslighting as heteronormative parents causing trans-children to doubt their desire to transgender. For example, instead of parents questioning a child's decision to adopt a non-binary, fluid gender identity they should be positive and celebrate the fact. The Urban Dictionary describes gaslighting as "A form of psychological abuse, sometimes called ambient abuse, where false information is presented to a victim, making them doubt their own memory, perception and quite often their sanity".

84. **Gay.** The 'Monash University Diversity and Inclusion Guide' defines Gay as "a person often a man, who

forms their primary loving and sexual relationships with others of the same gender". Gay is often used as a heteronormative insult by Cisgender people and, as a result, the line "gay your life must be" in 'Kookaburra Sits on the Old Gum Tree' has been changed to "Fun your life must be".

85. **Gaydar.** The 'OMG I'm Queer' booklet produced for the Safe Schools program defines 'gaydar' as the ability to tell if someone is gay. Students are warned, though, that "Unless you see someone sucking face with their same sex partner, or they tell you their sexuality, your gaydar isn't going to be exactly accurate".

86. **Gender.** The 'Gender Questioning' booklet defines gender as follows "Gender can refer to biological sex, social roles or gender identity. There are many genders, however the most commonly recognised are male or female". The authors go on to argue "There are no limitations on what your gender and identity can be". The academic behind the Safe Schools gender and sexuality program, Roz Ward, argues that gender is a social construct imposed by capitalism. Ward goes on the argue "Marxism offers both the hope and the strategy needed to create a world where human sexuality, gender and how we relate to our bodies can blossom in extraordinary new and amazing ways that we can only try to imagine today".

Any attempt to define gender in terms of a person's

biological sex at birth is considered oppressive and guilty of enforcing heteronormativity. After the Trump administration in America signalled that gender would be determined by one's genitalia at birth Sarah Warbelow, the legal director of the Human Rights Campaign which presses for the rights of lesbian, gay, bisexual and transgender people, argued "Transgender people are frightened... At every step where the administration has had the choice, they've opted to turn their back on transgender people."

The South Australian school curriculum some years ago, under the heading of 'Gender Equity', argues "Running through all the issues brought to light in investigating gender as a societal construct is the categorisation of the norm and the other with the other not being up to standard. Examples include the male/female, reason/emotion, sciences/humanities, public/private and paid/unpaid work splits. This persistent ordering into dichotomies shores up the norm in the dominant power relation to the other and is often not explicitly examined in curriculum, teaching and learning. Curriculum can continue to express these power relations or take part in their deconstruction and reconstruction".

87. **Gender deafness.** The Australian one time Foreign Affairs Minister Julie Bishop describes gender deafness as the way men during meetings, after ignoring a woman's contribution, accept what was said when the same point is made by a man. Peta Credlin, the Sky

News commentator and one time chief of staff to Prime Minister Abbott during the time Bishop was a minister in the Australian government, argues this never occurred in the cabinet room and describes Bishop's complaints as 'victim revisionism'.

88. **Gender fairy story book.** The author, Jo Hirst, describes this picture book as "designed for young children aged four years and up" that tells of a non-binary gender fairy who explains to children that "there are more identities than just male or female". Those committed to gender theory argue that traditional fairy tales like *Cinderella* and *Snow White* are guilty of heteronormativity as the happy ending privileges the love between a woman and a man.

The American actress Kristen Bell, after reading *Snow White* to her daughters, is reported as asking them "Don't you think that it's weird that the prince kisses Snow White without her permission? Because you cannot kiss someone if they're sleeping!". The British actress Keira Knightley is also concerned about the dangerous impact of traditional fairy tales and argues *Cinderella*, for example, portrays a girl unable to act decisively as she relies on the prince to rescue her.

89. **Gender identity.** The 'Sex Discrimination Amendment Act 2013' defines gender identity as "the gender-related identity, appearance or mannerisms or other

gender-related characteristics of a person (whether by way of medical intervention or not) without or without regard to the person's designated sex at birth". Material associated with the Safe Schools program argues that while you might be born with the physical characteristics of one of two sexes (girl or boy) there is no reason to believe this defines your gender. Gender is fluid and non-binary and how you express your gender is "a personal thing, everyone does it, and everyone does it differently". The Tasmanian parliament's lower house recently passed legislation allowing gender neutral birth certificates and also allowing teenagers over 16 to self-identify their gender simply by signing a statutory declaration.

90. **Gender mainstreaming.** The 'United Nations Entity for Gender Equality and the Empowerment of Women' describes this as "ensuring that gender perspectives and attention to the goal of gender equality are central to all activities - policy development, research, advocacy/dialogue, legislation, resource allocation, and planning, implementation and monitoring of programmes and projects".

91. **Gender neutral toilets.** Refers to any toilet, sometimes described as 'unisex', that does not specify male or female use. The Safe Schools booklet 'OMG I'M Trans' states that "Victoria has no explicit laws about using public bathrooms and you can use whichever ones you want". The Safe Schools booklet also argues that

schools should provide gender neutral toilets for boys and girls who self-identify other than their birth sex or who are in transition.

92. **Gender normative.** The belief that because the overwhelming majority of people self-identify as female or male that heterosexuality is the norm. The Meriam Webster dictionary defines gender normative as "adhering to or reinforcing ideal standards of masculinity or femininity". The 98% of Australians who self-identify as female or male are guilty of being gender normative.

93. **Gender pronouns/Inclusive language.** The Monash University guide to inclusive language recommends replacing gender specific pronouns like 'he' or 'she' with gender neutral alternatives like 'they' or 'zie'. Asking students their Christian name is also politically incorrect as the Monash guide argues "Terms like 'Christian name' should be replaced by 'first name' for the obvious reason that the person in question may not be Christian". The University of Melbourne's language guide goes one step further arguing that using the terms 'first name' and 'Christian name' reflects "a bias towards Christian, Anglo-Celtic culture". A Qantas staff guide recommends against using heteronormative descriptions like 'husband' and 'wife', preferring instead 'spouse' or 'partner'.

94. **Genderless fashion.** As the expression suggests genderless fashion involves designing clothes and accessories that no longer adopt a binary, heteronormative and oppressive view of fashion where there are distinctive styles suited to women and men.

95. **Genderqueer.** The 'GLBTQ Encyclopedia' defines genderqueer individuals as those "who feel that their gender identities and/or gender expressions do not correspond to the gender assigned to them at birth, but who do not want to transition to the 'opposite' gender. Characterizing themselves as neither female nor male, as both, or as somewhere in between, genderqueers challenge binary constructions of gender and traditional images of transgender people". Other descriptions include gender diverse, transboi, boydyke, third gendered, bi-gendered, multi-gendered, androgyne, and gender bender.

96. **Goosed.** According to the Urban Dictionary 'goosed' refers to being sexually molested or assaulted and the expression is common in the British acting industry. Dame Judi Dench, an unreconstructed Cisfemale, states when she first started acting being goosed behind the scenes was common and that "There was a time at the Old Vic when if you weren't goosed as you went in there was something wrong with you".

97. **Greenwash.** A term used to describe companies and corporations that disguise their environmental

destructive character by presenting themselves as ecologically sound and green. An example is the mining giant BHP marketing itself as dedicated to reducing greenhouse gas emissions while continuing to make profits from coal and petroleum.

98. **Guides by the side.** See 'facilitators'.

99. **Hate speech/hate crime.** The NSW Parliament describes hate speech as publicly threatening or inciting violence on the grounds of protected attributes such as race, religious affiliation, sexual orientation, gender identity and intersex or HIV/AIDS status. At the commonwealth level, under 18c of the Racial Discrimination Act, hate speech refers to "anything that is reasonably likely in all the circumstances to offend, insult, humiliate or intimidate on the grounds of race". Such is the force of the political correctness movement and identity politics that anyone who infringes the protected attributes is liable to be fined, imprisoned or made to suffer the consequences of what can be a lengthy and expensive legal process.

In Tasmania a transgender activist lodged a complaint with the Human Rights Commission against the Catholic Archbishop Julian Porteous for circulating a booklet detailing the Church's views about marriage. In Queensland three students underwent a lengthy, expensive and very public ordeal for complaining about not being able to use a computer centre set aside for indigenous students. The example of the conservative newspaper columnist Andrew Bolt being convicted for questioning the veracity of individuals claiming Aboriginal heritage also demonstrates how accusing people of so-called hate speech is being used to curtail free speech and enforce group think.

100. **Hegemony.** What appears natural or normal is often not the case and hegemony refers to how those in control of capitalist society are able to dominate others by conditioning them to accept their inferior and less privileged position. This can be achieved either by economic and political control or more subtly through controlling what happens in education, the marketplace and the media (Also see agitprop and false consciousness). In order to win the revolution the Italian Marxist Antonio Gramsci argued it was vital that activists took control of education to counter the hegemonic influence exerted by the state.

101. **Heteronormativity.** The 'OMG My Friends Queer' booklet associated with the Safe Schools program defines this as the "assumption that everyone is straight". Although approximately 98% of Australians according to one national survey self-identify as male or female LGBTIQ+ advocates argue it is wrong to assume that being heterosexual is normal. The University of Illinois Library describes heteronormativity as "a form of power and control that applies pressure to both straight and gay individuals through institutional arrangements

and accepted social norms".

102. **Heterosexism.** The Monash 'Inclusive Language Guide', under Glossary, describes this as referring to "the individual, group or institutional norms and behaviours that result from the assumption that all people are heterosexual, assuming heterosexuality is inherently normal or superior".

103. **Heterosexuality.** When discussing the concept of compulsory heterosexuality the encyclopedia of glbtq culture defines this as "the assumption that women and men are innately attracted to each other emotionally and sexually and that heterosexuality is normal and universal". Societies that endorse the love between a woman and a man are condemned because the "institutionalization of heterosexuality in our society leads to an institutionalized inequality of power".

Ignored is that if humanity is to survive men and women need to be attracted to one another for the purpose of procreation. Also ignored is the reality that the overwhelming majority of babies are either born female (XX chromosomes) or male (XY). Also ignored is Camille Paglia's assertion that much of 2nd and 3rd wave feminism is puritanical and that it's OK and natural to express one's sexuality.

104. **Homophobia.** The Safe Schools material defines this as the "fear, hatred or ignorance towards same

sex attracted people and people who are attracted to more than one gender. Homophobia usually leads to discrimination or abuse, like using the phrase 'that's so gay'". The definition is a broad one and, as a result, those who are heteronormative and defend marriage as between a woman and a man are often attacked as homophobic. After the tennis legend Margaret Court argued against same sex marriage and transgenderism another tennis legend Martina Navratilova condemned her as " a racist and a homophobe".

105. **Horizontally challenged.** The politically correct description instead of being labelled fat or overweight. Alternatives include 'differently sized' and having 'an alternative body image' (Also see fat shaming).

106. **Ideology.** Roger Scruton in *Culture Counts,* when discussing the meaning of ideology and drawing on Karl Marx, defines ideology as "a collection of ideas that have no authority in themselves but which disguise and mystify the social reality". Terry Eagleton in *Literary Theory* describes ideology as "the ways in which what we say and believe connects with the power-structure and power relations of the society we live in". Radical second and third wave feminists argue that young girls and women are conditioned by a patriarchal, misogynist ideology to accept their inferior roles as wives and mothers.

107. **Ideological state apparatus.** Made famous by Louis Althusser the expression refers to the way capitalist economies maintain power and are able to reproduce themselves. Althusser differentiates between a repressive state apparatus and an ideological one; the second involves institutions associated with religion, the education system, family, and political, legal and cultural systems. Taken together they enforce the ruling ideology by conditioning citizens to accept as natural or beneficial what is oppressive and exploitive.

In education the cultural-left argues competition and meritocracy where ability is rewarded disguises the fact that the system is designed to reinforce disadvantage and inequality as only those already privileged succeed.

108. **Identity history.** Stuart Macintyre in *The History Wars* details the rise of what he describes as "history from below" during the 1960s and 1970s; a time when history teaching began to focus on "social movements formed around sexuality, race and ethnicity". Instead of dealing with mainstream events, movements and individuals Macintyre argues minority groups assumed centre stage; leading to a situation where "identity history has been practised widely over the last two decades".

109. **Identity Politics.** Michael Gove associates the emergence of identity politics with the cultural-revolution of the late 60s and early 70s and the

influence of critical theory. Instead of individuals being part of a broader community with common interests they identify as one of the numerous victim groups oppressed and marginalised by capitalism and Western civilisation. The argument that LGBTIQ+ people, people of colour and women deserve positive discrimination simply because of their unique identity is an example of identity politics. Instead of being judged according to their character, as Martin Luther King Jr argued in his 'I have a dream' speech, such individuals portray themselves as victims because of their religion, race, gender, class or sexuality.

110. **Incels.** Short for "involuntary celibate", incels refers to those men who share in common an inability to attract and be comfortable with women. The urban dictionary describes incels as "a person (usually male) who has a horrible personality and treats women like sexual objects and thinks his lack of a sex life comes from being 'ugly' when it's really just his blatant sexism and terrible attitude".

111. **Intersectionality.** A paper delivered at the '22nd International Summit on Violence, Abuse and Trauma' held in California describes intersectionality as "overlapping or intersecting social identities and related systems of oppression, domination and/or discrimination". Identities that can intersect include "gender, race, social class, ethnicity, nationality, sexual orientation, religion, age, mental disability, physical

disability, mental illness and physical illness, etc". The urban dictionary defines intersectionality as "an all-you-can-eat buffet of mental illnesses and victim statuses". An example of intersectionality is an individual who is vertically challenged, queer, non-white and experiencing mental and physical disabilities.

The international Women's Development Agency describes 'Intersectionality' as "acknowledging the interplay between gender and other forms of discrimination, like race, age, class, socioeconomic status, physical or mental ability, gender or sexual identity, religion, or ethnicity. The barriers faced by a middle class woman living in Melbourne are not the same as those of a queer woman living in rural Fiji. Women aren't just exposed to sexism – racism, ableism, ageism, homophobia, transphobia and religious persecution are intrinsically linked to how they experience inequality".

112. **Islamophobic.** Mehmet Ozaip on the Conversation website defines Islamophobia as a special form of racism revealing "indiscriminate negative attitudes or emotions directed at Islam and Muslims. An Islamophobic incident is any act comprising of abusive hatred, vilification and violence inflicted on Muslims going about their daily lives". Based on this definition anyone who criticises the Koran for advocating a jihad against the West or for sanctioning the mistreatment of women is islamophobic. One example is the Somalian

Muslim female Ayaan Hirsi Ali who is condemned as an islamophobe for daring to argue in her book *Heretic* that "Islam is not a religion of peace".

113. **In bed with a wog.** An obsolete expression once used to describe being in bed because of catching a cold or the flu. Now considered an example of unconscious racism as 'wog' is a description that demeans and offends Italians as well as people from Asia (otherwise known as Worthy Oriental Gentlemen).

114. **Intersex.** The Monash University 'Inclusive Language Guide' defines intersex as including "a variety of biological conditions; intersex people are born with physical, hormonal or genetic features that are neither wholly female nor wholly male; or a combination of female and male; or neither female nor male".

115. **Jazz hands.** According to the UK Daily Mail the student union at the University of Manchester is asking students to show appreciation and enjoyment by Jazz hands as the loud and intrusive noise and movement caused by clapping might trigger anxiety and alarm.

116. **Judeo-Christianity.** While Pope Francis uses the expression to stress the close association between the Jewish and Christian faiths the Australian historian Tony Taylor describes Judeo-Christianity as a "fabricated myth". A myth used by conservatives when arguing the Old and New Testaments are fundamental to any

understanding of what constitutes Western civilisation.

117. **Keep it up.** An expression once widely used to motivate and encourage but is now considered politically incorrect as it is considered phallocentric and misogynist as it appears to privilege the sex act from a male perspective.

118. **Knowledge navigators.** See 'digital natives'.

119. **Lesbophobia.** Preferred by those who argue the word 'homophobia' is unacceptable as using the prefix 'homo' privileges men and is guilty of phallocentrism.

120. **LGBTIQ+.** An acronym used to describe Lesbian, Gay, Bisexual, Transgender, Intersex, Queer and 'plus' people. In the journal *English in Australia* (Vol. 53. No. 2) the editors explain using the symbol + acknowledges "these bounded labels are fluid and not exhaustive; they do not capture the complexities of time and place. It also works to include the other/future non-conforming identities". As to what these future non-conforming identities are we can only guess.

121. **LINO.** Liberals in name only is an Australian political expression similar to the American RINO – Republicans in name only. It refers to those in the centre rightLiberal Party who instead of supporting conservative beliefs and values argue for centre left polices similar to the Australian Labor Party.

122. **Literature.** An arcane and elitist category of texts usually referring to those plays, poems, short stories and novels that have something lasting and profound to say about human nature and the world in which we live. Terry Eagleton in *Literary Theory an Introduction* details the impact of theory and notes we cannot assume that what is "currently termed 'literature' will always and everywhere be the most important focus of attention". Eagleton goes as far as suggesting "Anything can be literature, and anything that can be regarded unalterably and unquestionably literature – Shakespeare for example – can cease being literature".

The politically correct alternative 'texts' is now preferred, defined by the Australian national curriculum as anything communicated in "written, spoken, visual, multimodal, and in print or digital/online forms. Multimodal texts combine language with other means of communication such as visual images, soundtrack or spoken words, as in film or computer presentation media". As a result, in English classes students are allowed to study multi-media texts and other forms of communication including SMS texts, graffiti and movie posters. A lecturer responsible for teaching prospective English teachers once noted that the class had a very productive time deconstructing a tissue box as a text.

123. **MAGA.** An acronym standing for Make America Great Again and associated with President Trump and his supporters. Jussie Smollett, a black gay American actor

who staged a fake episode of hate crime, had one of the attackers cry "This is MAGA country". The fact that mainstream media was so quick to describe the made up incident as true and an example of white racism is an example of politically correct fake news (otherwise known as agitprop).

124. **Male.** A binary, heteronormative description that privileges and normalises masculinity to the exclusion of other more liberating and authentic forms of LGBTIQ+ gender and sexuality.

125. **Male assigned at birth.** Used to describe an individual's birth-sex on the basis, instead of being biologically determined, that traditional binary sex categories are restrictive social constructs imposed on innocent and unsuspecting babies by a heteronormative, transphobic society.

126. **Male colonisation.** Nikki Gemmell condemns the publishers Allen and Unwin for choosing a male journalist to write about the #MeToo movement as an example of "men colonising women's domains". Gemmell describes the #MeToo movement as "courageous, fraught, intensely female" and argues that asking a man to write about the issue is simply another example of "structural sexism" where men are privileged and given preferential treatment over women.

127. **Man box.** A journalist at *The Fairfax Press*, Anna Prytz, describes a man box as when men are hemmed in and constrained because they believe "that men should be unemotional, hyper-sexual, physically tough, stoic and in control". Men being brave, sexually active, physically strong and in control of their emotions is politically incorrect as such attributes are binary in nature and ignore the need for men to be more in touch with their feminine and LGBTIQ+ side. Also see Toxic Masculinity.

128. **Manhole.** A description that reinforces male dominance. Alternatives include 'personnel access structure', 'femhole' or 'utility hole'. The Berkeley City Council in California mandates in its municipal code that 'manhole' be replaced by 'maintenance hole'.

129. **Manshaming.** Describes the process of unfairly attacking and criticising men and making them feel guilty because they are men – usually, but not always, involves second and third wave feminists. School programs dealing with domestic violence like Respectful Relationships present men as violent and dangerous without any acknowledgement that not all men are guilty. The Gillette video 'Is this the best a man can get?' has also been criticised for presenting a biased and one-sided view of men.

Another example involves Victoria's Assistant Commissioner of Police Luke Cornelius who in response to the appalling and distressing murder of Courtney

Herron in Melbourne describes all men as guilty. Even though the alleged psychotic male responsible acted alone and it was late at night in an isolated park on being interviewed Cornelius argues "The key point is (that) this is men's behaviour, it's not about women's behaviour".

130. **Mansplaining.** Refers to those men who treat women as unintelligent and incapable of understanding by being condescending and patronizing. The University of Adelaide was recently criticised for a billboard showing a man seated surrounded by a number of women passively listening while he held centre stage talking.

131. **Mansplaying.** Refers to the way men and boys maximise their seating space on public transport by sitting with their legs open as wide as possible. Also seen by radical feminists as an unwarranted and offensive display of male dominance and of phallocentrism.

132. **Marriage.** Historically and across cultures marriage has been defined as the union of a woman and a man for the purpose of procreation and the survival of the species. Cultural-left critics, on the other hand, argue marriage is a relationship that institutionalises the oppression and mistreatment of women. Marriage, instead of being reciprocal is an institution invented by patriarchal societies for the benefit of men. Radical feminists consider sex within marriage as a form of

exploitation except if you are gay, lesbian, trans, intersex or queer where getting married is a form of liberation that publicly validates gayness/queerness.

As argued by Neel Burton in Psychology Today "On the marriage market, women are made to feel like low value, perishable goods. To find a taker, whether for marriage or just for sex, they need, much more than men, to conform to sexist, ageist, and racist stereotypes, and do appalling things such as wear makeup and high heels, which become the visible symbols of their oppression". Some feminists equate marriage with prostitution on the basis that both involve subjugation and sexual exploitation by men in what is a phallocentric, male dominated society.

133. **Meme.** The Oxford dictionary defines a 'meme' as "An element of a culture or system of behaviour passed from one individual to another by imitation or other non-genetic means". For example, as a result of watching the film *Birdbox* thousands around the world competed to wear blindfolds in challenging situations. Such was the danger that Netflix issued a statement "Can't believe I have to say this, but: PLEASE DO NOT HURT YOURSELVES WITH THIS BIRD BOX CHALLENGE. We don't know how this started, and we appreciate the love, but Boy and Girl have just one wish for 2019 and it is that you not end up in the hospital due to memes".

134. **#MeToo movement.** An international movement against sexual assault and harassment initially sparked by the Harvey Weinstein scandal but that now provides a world-wide platform to identify and punish men guilty of such offenses. While applauded in Hollywood as justifiable the French actress Catherine Deneuve signed an open letter with 99 other women in criticising the #MeToo movement for being puritanical and guilty of treating women as passive and always the victim in their relationships with men.

135. **#MenToo.** The Australian author Bettina Arndt in her book *#MenToo* argues that in the West we are living in an anti-male society where men are demonised and treated unfairly by radical feminists and gender warriors. In areas like family divorce, domestic violence and youth suicide Arndt argues men's rights are considered secondary to those of women.

136. **Microaggression.** In addition to obvious forms of aggression and victimisation microaggression refers to those politically incorrect acts, while never intending to be offensive, that are calculated to insult victim groups. One example that went viral around the internet is when the then Leader of the Opposition Julia Gillard in parliament labelled the Australian Prime Minister Tony Abbott as misogynist for looking at his watch while she was giving a speech condemning him as hostile to women.

137. **Misandry.** Involves unfairly criticising or condemning men and boys by presenting a stereotype that paints males as misogynist, sexist, violent and exploitive.

138. **Misgendering.** In the words of a language guide prepared by the Australian Defence Force Academy misgendering involves incorrectly addressing LGBTIQ+ personnel by using heteronormative pronouns like 'he' or 'she' when such personnel self-identify as the opposing gender. The guide states using language that fails to respect the gender identity of those being addressed "can have a significant effect on transgender individuals as it is often an expression of a lack of understanding of acceptance of that person's identity". A famous Australian example involves Major Gaynor Sr being warned about continuing to use a male pronoun when addressing a fellow officer who transitioned to become a woman (now known as Cate McGregor).

139. **Misspeaking.** The description used when you suddenly realise what you have said or are halfway through saying is politically incorrect and you have entered the killing zone. The British Labour politician Angela Smith when talking about non-white people described them as having a "funny tin.." before stopping and apologising for misspeaking. The assumption is she was about to say "tint" or "tinge".

140. **Motherhood.** An exploitive and heteronormative concept imposed by patriarchal societies to restrict women to childbearing and remaining dependent on men. Andrea O'Reilly in 'Outlaw(ing) Motherhood: A Theory and Politic of Maternal Empowerment for the Twenty-First Century' describes motherhood as an example of "gender essentialism" that disempowers and oppresses women and argues "Only by unearthing and severing the ideological underpinning of patriarchal motherhood, gender essentialism, can we develop a politic of maternal empowerment and a practice of outlaw motherhood for the twenty-first century".

141. **Misogynist.** A term used to describe men who exhibit and demonstrate a hostility and dislike towards women. Berit Brogaard in Psychology Today argues misogyny is often unconscious and that "Women haters (unconsciously) get off on treating women badly. Every time they can put down a woman or hurt her feelings, they unconsciously feel good because deep down in their hidden brain, their bad behavior is rewarded with a dose of the pleasure chemical dopamine —which makes them want to repeat the behaviour again and again".

142. **Misogyny.** Defined as the hatred, dislike mistrust or prejudice that men feel towards women. According to the Victorian Government's Respectful Relationships material men are inherently violent towards women on the basis that one of the principal causes of violence

against women is "a traditional view about gender roles and relationships". The argument is put that "men who are hostile towards women's non-conformity to gender roles and to challenges to male authority have a particular tendency towards violence". Ignored is that other significant causes of domestic violence include poverty and drug and alcohol abuse.

143. **Misogynoir.** Attributed to the black, queer, feminist scholar Moya Bailey this refers to a form of abuse directed at black women that stems from the intersectionality of misogyny and racism. The *Herald Sun* cartoonist Mark Knight's depiction of Serena Williams abusing the umpire and smashing her tennis racket during the US Open Tennis final is politically incorrect as it is guilty, supposedly, of presenting Williams as a black, angry woman.

144. **Mother's Day.** See Father's Day.

145. **Multiculturalism.** Multiculturalism, unlike integration, involves treating all cultures as equal except for Western culture that is seen as Eurocentric, oppressive and guilty of 'whiteness'. The Australian Civics and Citizenship curriculum describes Australia as a "diverse and dynamic society" and "and a "secular nation with a multi-cultural and multi-faith society".

146. **Nanny state.** Refers to governments interfering and taking control of people's lives based on the premise that citizens are incapable of looking after themselves and being responsible. Because of political correctness governments have become even more protective on the assumption that the state knows best and must be the final arbiter. One Australian example relates to aviation firefighters not being able to use ladders over 2 metres high for safety reasons. Another example involves local governments banning monkey bars in playgrounds because they put children at risk and schools stopping children doing cartwheels in the playground.

147. **Nativity scenes.** Once a widely accepted way to celebrate Christmas and the birth of Christ but now see as divisive and unacceptable as Australia is a multi-faith, multi-cultural, multi-ethnic society. It is wrong to privilege what is a Eurocentric, Christian event as all cultures and all religions deserve equal treatment. Leading up to Christmas it is increasingly common for local councils and schools to ban nativity scenes as they are seen as offensive to non-Christians.

148. **Nip in the air.** An expression once used to describe feeling cold but now considered politically incorrect as it is offensive to those of Japanese origin. Alternatives include 'a chill in the air' and 'being physically inconvenienced as a result of suboptimal temperature'.

149. **No-platforming.** Refers to the practice of denying politically incorrect speakers the right to speak publicly at events because their views are deemed offensive and unacceptable. The feminist Germaine Greer was no platformed in the UK at a university event because she argues a man who transitions to become a woman can never be a woman. The Australian Bettina Arndt also faces opposition when trying to talk at universities because she argues men are often discriminated against in favour of women in areas like divorce proceedings and domestic violence. Arndt also argues the prevalence of female students being sexually harassed on university campuses is overstated.

150. **Non-animalist language.** The People for the Ethical Treatment of Animals (PETA) condemns language that oppresses and commodifies animals and produces resources for schools to help children be more caring and sensitive. Examples include:

Politically incorrect	Non-animalist
Kill two birds with one stone	Feed two birds with one stone
Let the cat out of the bag	Spill the beans
Take the bull by the horns	Take the flower by the thorns
Be a guinea pig	Be a test tube
Bring home the bacon	Bring home the bagels
More than one way to skin a cat	More than one way to skin a potato

151. **Non-gender normative/non-heteronormative.** According to a paper published in *English in Australia* (Vol.53. No.2) titled 'Textual Constraints: Queering the

Senior English Text List in the Australian Curriculum' the overwhelming majority of selected texts for senior school students deal with heteronormative, binary characters, themes and relationships. The paper argues to rectify the imbalance there must be more texts embracing a definition of gender and sexuality that is fluid and dynamic. Texts that are non-gender normative and non-heteronormative.

152. **Oppositional defiance disorder.** It's no longer acceptable for teachers to label students as disruptive or to punish them for offensive behaviour. Such students are suffering from Oppositional Defiance Disorder and are not responsible for their actions. Instead of being punished or reprimanded such students are entitled to additional resources and a personalised curriculum to ensure they are treated fairly, not discriminated against and given the opportunity to reach their full potential.

153. **Orientalism.** Roger Scruton attributes this expression to Edward Said and describes it as denoting the West's attitude to the Middle East. One that suggests a "denigrating and patronizing attitude towards eastern civilizations" and that portrays the Middle East as "a world of wan indifference and vaporous intoxication".

154. **Pansexual.** The Them website defines pansexual as "someone who is attracted to people of all genders — not just cisgender and transgender men and women, but nonbinary people, gender-nonconforming people,

and anyone whose genders fall outside of the gender binary, or beyond traditional definitions of what it means to be a 'man' or 'woman'". An extreme example of someone who is pansexual is Calum Jones who describes himself as "a heteroflexible pansexual solo polyamorous relationship anarchist".

155. **Partner.** A term once used to describe those working together in business or commerce but now the preferred gender neutral term for those who are married or living in a long term relationship.

156. **Patriarchal.** Second and third wave feminists argue that Western society is ruled by men who subjugate and dominate women. There is no equality between the sexes as institutions like marriage force women to be chattels exploited by men. The Australian feminist Dale Spender sees patriarchy in every aspect and structure of society, a situation where "I am using patriarchy in all of these senses; I am using it as in inclusive term to encompass a sex-class system, and a symbolic system which supports male supremacist social arrangements. That is why I see patriarchy everywhere; there is no aspect of our lives, that I know of, which is outside patriarchy". The language we use is not immune and in 'Man Made Society', Spender argues "Every aspect of the language from its structure to the conditions of its use must be scrutinised if we are to detect both the blatant and the subtle means by which the edifice of male supremacy has been assembled".

157. **Pets.** 'The Journal of Animal Ethics', edited by Reverend Professor Andrew Linzey, argues the term 'pets' is unacceptable as it demeans and commodifies animals. The alternative description is 'companion animals' – otherwise known as 'non-human, sentient creatures'.

158. **Phallic teacher.** Lucinda McKnight from Deakin University refers to Phallacism as worshipping the phallus (penis) and describes the phallic teacher as "the empowered, high quality, tool-wielding teacher discursively created by a neoliberal educational regime". McKnight argues incorporating an evidence-based approach to teaching and using standardised tests to measure performance is guilty of preferencing "masculinist authority".

159. **Pink washing.** An expression employed by the LGBTIQ+ community to describe those corporations, businesses and politicians who pretend to be friendly and supportive in order to appear progressive and non-binary while still being heteronormative and guilty of homophobia and transphobia (see virtue signaling).

160. **Postmodernism.** The Stanford Encyclopedia of Philosophy describes postmodernism as "a set of critical, strategic and rhetorical practices employing concepts such as difference, repetition, the trace, the simulacrum, and hyperreality to destabilize other concepts such as presence, identity, historical progress, epistemic certainty, and the univocity of meaning".

There are no truths we can agree on as how each person relates to others and perceives the wider world is relative and subjective. Except of course for the belief that postmodernism is the only correct way to interpret and understand one's identity and one's place in the world.

Richard Tarnes describes postmodernism as the belief "that human knowledge is subjectively determined by a multitude of factors; that objective essences, or things-in-themselves, are neither accessible nor positable... The critical search for truth is constrained to be tolerant of ambiguity and pluralism, and its outcome will necessarily be knowledge that is relative and fallible rather than absolute or certain".

161. **Poststructuralism.** Similar to postmodernism, poststructuralism denies the referential quality of language and the inherent meaning of texts. Terry Eagleton in *Literary Theory an Introduction* makes the point "If meaning, the signified, was a passing product of words or signifiers, always shifting and unstable, part-present and part-absent, how could there be any determinate truth or meaning at all?". Taken to its logical conclusion poststructuralism makes it impossible to engage in rational discussion and debate as arguments and opinions are incapable of being objectively tested or verified.

162. **Pansexual.** An individual who is neither Cisfemale nor Cismale but who enjoys being romantically and physically involved with individuals of all genders and sexes.

163. **Pregnant person.** According to Melbourne based The Equality Institute it is unacceptable to use the description 'pregnant women' as limiting childbirth to women is an unfair and discriminatory binary, heteronormative concept. The Institute recommends "try using the phrase 'Pregnant people' because people of all genders can fall pregnant". The Institute goes on to argue "Consider all people when using language — including trans and non-binary folk — and ensure that your language is inclusive of everyone, when talking about pregnancy or anything else. Language matters". The City of Berkeley in California also recommends using the description "pregnant employees" as opposed to "pregnant women" in order to recognise the importance of "non-binary gender inclusivity".

164. **Phallocentric.** Taken from the Greek 'phallus' – meaning 'penis' and 'centric' – meaning 'centred on'; feminists argue that Western society is phallocentric in nature as men are privileged whereas women are treated as inferior and ripe for exploitation. Pointing a finger when making a statement or presenting an argument is an example of being phallocentric and the politically correct alternative for those who are Woke is to hold out one's hand with the palm upwards.

165. **Positive discrimination.** Based on the belief that as Western, capitalist societies systematically oppress and disadvantage marginalised groups the only solution is to positively discriminate in favour of victim groups and oppressed individuals in order to ensure equality of outcomes. Instead of relying on merit and ability the PC alternative it to mandate equal gender representation in areas like corporate boards and preselection for election to parliament.

166. **Post-colonial theory.** Drawing on Edward Said's book *Orientalism* this refers to the way Western imperial powers justify colonialism and the accompanying violence and exploitation by describing it as a 'civilising mission'. Those cultures invaded are defined through Western eyes as inferior and described as uncivilised and representing the 'the Other' to justify their mistreatment. Critics of Western countries guilty of imperialism rarely, if ever, mention the role Islam played in its invasion and subjugation of other countries and territories.

167. **Queer Theory.** Drawing on the French academic and psychologist Foucault and in opposition to categories like 'gay' and 'lesbian', queer theory posits that gender and sexuality are social constructs and, as a result, resist any clear or definite definition. The Stanford Encyclopedia of Philosophy, under the heading Homosexuality, suggests "In contrast to gay or lesbian, 'queer,' it is argued, does not refer to an essence, whether

of a sexual nature or not. Instead it is purely relational, standing as an undefined term that gets its meaning precisely by being that which is outside of the norm, however that norm itself may be defined". The author goes on to quote David M. Halperin's definition "Queer is ... whatever is at odds with the normal, the legitimate, the dominant. There is nothing in particular to which it necessarily refers. It is an identity without an essence".

168. **Reproductive coercion.** The Children by Choice website suggests reproductive coercion is just as widespread as rape and defines it as "an easy and effective and cowardly way of manipulating and controlling a woman by limiting her autonomy over her fertility and reproductive health and choices". Examples include a man refusing to wear a condom during sexual intercourse and a man forcing a woman to become pregnant.

169. **Reverse racism.** While some dislike the term (on the basis that racism is racism regardless of the target) the expression is used to denote an unfair prejudice and bias against a society's dominant race. An example of reverse racism is the assumption that all white people are privileged and incapable of accepting non-whites as equals (see Whiteness and White supremacism).

170. **Revenge feminism.** *The Australian* newspaper's Janet Albrechtsen describes this extreme form of feminism as "one part of a larger body of grievance

politics" influenced by postmodern theory that argues knowledge is a social construct and that all relationships are based on power and privilege. Western society is inherently misogynist and patriarchal and all men are guilty of oppressing and enslaving women.

171. **Santa Claus.** A mythical figure used to delude children often with the hope of making them better behaved and to foster a commitment to materialism and consumerism. Rebecca English from the Queensland University of Technology argues "You shouldn't lie about Santa because you are encouraging your children, usually with made-up proof, to believe a morally ambiguous lie. I'm not alone in being devastated learning of my parents' elaborate deceit about Santa, leaving me to wonder what other lies they had told".

172. **Safe Spaces.** Universities now have Safe Spaces to ensure there are havens for those oppressed by the Eurocentric, heteronormative, racist and sexist environment that prevails on campuses and in lectures and tutorials. University of Sydney Women's Officer Madeline Ward argues "safe spaces such as the on-campus Queer Space and the Wom*n's Room and ethno cultural room for 'people of colour' were necessary". Ward argues "I would say the queer and ethno spaces are vital because society is racist and homophobic". (*Daily Telegraph* 9th August 2018).

The University of Southern Queensland's library

policy on providing Safe Spaces states the university is committed to providing "a visible and inclusive safe area for staff and students who identify as lesbian, gay, bisexual, transgender, intersex or queer (LGBTIQ)". The policy goes on to state "Our LGBTIQ community can be assured that the Libraries are a designated safe space for LGBTIQ students and staff to work and study, free from harassment or discrimination based on sexuality, gender identity or gender expression".

173. **Safe Schools.** Contrary to the argument Safe Schools is an anti-bullying program Roz Ward, who helped design the program, admits "Safe Schools Coalition is about supporting gender and sexual diversity, not about stopping bullying". She says it's about "sexual diversity, about same sex attraction, about being transgender, about being lesbian, gay, bisexual – say the words transgender, intersex". As with much of radical gender theory the ideology underpinning Safe Schools is heavily influenced by Marxism. Ward argues "only Marxism provides the theory and practice of genuine human liberation" and "it will only be through a revitalized class struggle and revolutionary change that we can hope for the liberation of LGBTI people".

174. **Seahorse dad.** A description of a woman who undergoes gender transition to become a man but who still wants to give birth to a child. The journalist Freddy McConnell who was able to conceive is the subject of the film *Seahorse* and the film's director Jeanie Finlay

argues it's OK for a transman to give birth as "Lots of people want to have a baby... it's a natural thing".

175. **Sexist.** While the Urban Dictionary suggests anyone can be sexist according to second and third wave feminists men are the worst offenders. Men are inherently sexist as they demean and objectify women as sexual objects and, unless properly conditioned, boys follow in their father's footsteps.

176. **Shadowbanning.** A form of censorship whereby a person's activity on a social networking site is curtailed or limited without their knowledge. In America Republican politicians and some conservative commentators accuse Twitter and Facebook of restricting access to their accounts by manipulating search engines and what is posted as to make it difficult, if not impossible, for them to be found by others using the internet.

177. **Sheila.** An offensive and outdated expression once used by Australian men to describe women. As in "she's a bonza sheila".

178. **Sensitivity tool kits.** See Diversity Tool Kits.

179. **Sexuality.** Material associated with the Safe Schools program *OMG I'm Queer* argues that a person's sexuality is not determined by one's sex at birth rather it is fluid and subjective. "All people have their own

sexuality. Whether that's straight, gay, queer, bisexual or something completely different; each person's sexuality applies only to them". The American College of Paediatricians, on the other hand, argue sexuality is binary in nature as "sexuality is an objective biological binary trait "XY" and "XX" are genetic markers of male and female, respectively – not genetic markers of a disorder. The norm for human design is to be conceived either male or female. Human sexuality is binary by design with the obvious purpose being the reproduction and flourishing of our species. This principle is self-evident".

180. **Short shaming.** Dan Kaufman in *The Age* newspaper complains about the prejudice displayed against short men in what is "a heightist world". Women prefer men who are tall, research shows short men are made to do more housework and expressions like "short changed" and "falling short" cause further harm.

181. **Slut shaming.** After announcing her intention not to recontest her parliamentary seat the Australian Labor Party's Emma Hussar stated she was forced to resign because of "slut shaming". Leora Tanenbaum in the HuffPost describes this as "the experience of being labeled a sexually out-of-control girl or woman (a "slut" or "ho") and then being punished socially for possessing this identity. Slut-shaming is sexist because only girls and women are called to task for their sexuality, whether real or imagined; boys and men are congratulated for

the exact same behavior. This is the essence of the sexual double standard Boys will be boys, and girls will be sluts".

182. **Snowflakes.** Refers to recent generations of young people who lack confidence and resilience and who are easily offended and upset if confronted by what they consider politically incorrect. Trigger warnings and Safe Spaces exist to protect snowflakes as do politically correct concepts like identity politics and victimhood.

Young children are so anxious and concerned about missing out that a school in Sydney has banned birthday cards. A notice sent home to parents states, "At the request of parents, and in consultation with the school community, Mosman Public School has asked that student birthday party invitations are not handed out during school hours due to the distress caused to students seen not to be invited".

183. **Space invader.** During a recent Australian federal election campaign television debate where Prime Minister Scott Morrison walked towards and closed in on the then Leader of the Opposition Bill Shorten, Shorten complained Morrison was a 'space invader'. Space invaders are those who impose their physical presence on others denying them the right to private space and the need to feel safe and not threatened.

184. **Speciesism.** Animal rights activists argue that speciesism, similar to racism, sexism, homophobia and transphobia, involves those who see themselves as superior and who discriminate against and exploit 'the Other' – in this case non-human sentient creatures. As stated by Germain Greer on hearing about the Australian naturalist film maker Steve Irwin being killed by a stingray "The animal world has finally taken its revenge".

185. **Structural sexism.** Drawing on critical theory the argument is that even though women might be comfortable with their roles in society and feel they are treated fairly, the reality is society is inherently sexist and oppressive. The way society is structured, especially institutions like the family, education and work, conditions women to accept an inferior role while men dominate.

The Marxist inspired feminist Shulamith Firestone argues that the only way for women to achieve true freedom and equality is to radically reshape society by making men redundant. She writes in 'The Dialectic Of Sex' "the end goal of the feminist revolution must be, unlike that of the first feminist movement, not just the elimination of male privilege but of the sex distinction itself, genital differences between human beings would no longer matter culturally".

186. **SWERF** (Sex-work exclusionary radical feminist). Refers to those feminists opposed to the sex industry as prostitution involves women being commodified and treated as sexual objects by men.

187. **TERF** (Trans exclusionary radical feminist). Described as a Ciswoman who intentionally offends transpeople by arguing that gender and sexuality are binary and that a man cannot transition to becoming a woman. In the English town of Macclesfield a transperson after being confronted by a women with a t-shirt with the words "Women: noun adult human female" argued "When you're trying to relax in your fave pub and there is a TERF wearing an anti-trans T-shirt... it's disgusting and I'm so upset by it".

188. **TCE.** Refers to Traditional Cultural Expression. Brigitte Vezina in 'Curbing Cultural Appropriation in the Fashion Industry' criticises those in the West's fashion industry guilty of cultural appropriation by copying the designs and fabrics associated with non-white cultures. Examples include the American company Urban Outfitters producing clothing based on Navajo Nation motifs and designs and a French designer copying a traditional blouse worn by the Mixe people – an indigenous Mexican community. Vezina argues traditional cultural expression should be protected by enforcing intellectual property rights.

189. **The missus.** A misogynist and patriarchal expression used by husbands to describe their wives. Equally as offensive are descriptions like 'she who must be obeyed' and the 'better half'. Wendy Tuohy in *The Age* argues a man using the expression treats his wife as a "person of lower status, over whom I have power and control, and whose opinions matter less than mine".

190. **The long march.** Roger Kimball in his book *The Long March* attributes the phrase to German New Leftist radical Rudi Dutschke active during the cultural revolution of the 60s and 70s and before him the Italian Marxist Antonio Gramsci. Instead of overthrowing Western societies and establishing a socialist utopia by direct means using violence and force the strategy is to infiltrate and take control of the institutions underpinning society. (See also 'critical theory', 'culture wars' and the 'Frankfurt School'). The expression the Long March is also associated with the communist dictator Chairman Mao who was responsible for the murder, torture, starvation and death of millions of Chinese during his reign of terror.

191. **Theory.** Associated with the cultural-left and the dominance of critical theory the term 'theory' refers to a rainbow alliance of theories, including: Marxism, neo-Marxism, feminist, gender, queer and post-colonial theories. While often in disagreement all see Western civilisation as oppressive and are directed at overthrowing capitalism and those institutions seen as

misogynist, heteronormative, racist, elitist and binary.

192. **The Other.** Drawing on critical theory and aspects of Orientalism 'the Other' refers to the way more dominant and powerful groups in society or nation states justify their crimes by labelling those being exploited and oppressed as 'the Other'. Categorising LGBTIQ+ people, women and people of colour as outside what is considered acceptable and normal makes it easier to justify their exclusion and mistreatment.

193. **Thicc.** Originating as a term used by African-Americans to describe women with voluptuous Rubens like figures and defined by the Urban Dictionary as a person who has "fat in the right places, creating sexy curves". After using the term 'Thicc' to describe a curvaceous sea otter a Californian aquarium was criticised for equating African-Americans with animals and for cultural appropriation.

194. **Toxic Masculinity.** Refers to masculine characteristics and qualities that second and third wave feminists argue are sexist, violent and misogynist. Toxic masculinity leads to sexual exploitation and commodification of women, domestic violence and men being insensitive and closed emotionally. Camille Paglia argues the expression is unfair as it demonstrates a "peevish, grudging rancour against men" where "men's faults, failings, and foibles have been seized on and magnified into gruesome bills of indictment".

195. **Transgender.** The Safe Schools 'Gender Questioning' booklet published by Gay and Lesbian Health Victoria & Rainbow Network Victoria describes transgender as referring to "a large range of people whose common experience is that their inner sense of gender is different to the sex they were assigned at birth". Gender is defined as fluid and limitless and the booklet states "There is no right or wrong in this, it's about figuring out what feels right for you".

196. **Transgender toilets.** The Hobart City Council is leading Australia with its plans to turn all male and female public toilets into transgender ones. Non-binary Hobart City councillor Holly Ewin argues trans-people are regularly attacked in gender binary public toilets and the move is about "positive reinforcement and breaking down stigmas around trans bodies". Bronwyn Williams, for the feminist group Women Speak Tasmania as reported in *The Australian* September 2019, is opposed to the idea. Williams expresses the fear that transgender toilets risk the likelihood of women and girls being accosted by biological males. Williams states "If I had daughters, I wouldn't be letting them go in by themselves if this sort of policy was in place".

197. **Transphobia.** The material associated with the Safe Schools gender and sexuality program defines transphobia as the "fear and hatred of gender diverse or transgender people, their desires and behaviours, that often leads to discrimination or abuse". Stopping boys

who self-identify as girls from using female toilets and change rooms in schools is an example of transphobia as is parents counselling their children against undergoing gender transition (see gaslighting).

Stopping transwomen from taking part in female sports is also an example of transphobia. A Canadian cyclist who was born as a man and who transitioned, Rachel McKinnon, argues anyone who complains Ciswomen in sport are disadvantaged is politically incorrect. McKinnon argues it's a human rights issue and not a matter of being physically advantaged "We shouldn't be worried about transpeople taking over the Olympics. We should be worried about their fairness and human rights instead".

Juliet Macur, in an article published in the *New York Times*, cites an opposing view given by Dr Eric Vilain who argues "Now I'm really worried about the future of women in sports because if we push this argument, anyone declaring a female gender can compete as a woman. We're moving toward one big competition, and the very predictable result of that competition is that there will be no women winners." The champion tennis player Martina Navratilova is also concerned arguing "It is surely unfair on women who have to compete against people, biologically, who are still men".

Even though a strong supporter of the LGBTIQ+ community Navratilova has been criticised for her comments by Rachael McKinnon, a world champion transgender cyclist, arguing on the LGBT website Out that Navratilova's comments are "disturbing, upsetting, and deeply transphobic".

198. **Transpeople.** The 'Gender Questioning' booklet suggests individuals have the right to identify as "being male, female, something other or in between" and that as a result they can be either "lesbian, gay, bisexual, queer, straight or something else". Words used to describe transpeople include: "Transwomen, Transman, Transguy, Trannyboy, boi, Trannygirl, Trans masculine, Trans feminine, Tranz, bi-gendered, third sex, poly gendered, transbutch, transfag, trannydyke, androgyne".

199. **Trigger warnings.** The British academic Frank Furedi describes how trigger warnings originated in universities and campuses in North America to protect snowflake students who might be offended by material encountered during their studies. Examples include poems, plays and novels that are "assigned a health warning to indicate that they contain scenes of domestic violence, sexism, racism or a variety of other pathologies". Examples include the Greek tragedy *Media* that involves domestic violence and filicide, Marvell's poem *To His Coy Mistress* that commodifies women and *Hamlet* where Ophelia commits suicide.

200. **Trolling/trolled.** Evita March on The Conversation website defines online trolling as "deceptive and disruptive online behaviour which typically involves posting inflammatory and malicious comments to deliberately provoke and upset people". An example of trolling involves the often racist and offensive online remarks directed at Meghan Markle causing her friend George Clooney to go public saying "she has been pursued and vilified and chased in the same way that Diana was and it's history repeating itself".

201. **Trump derangement syndrome.** Fareed Zakaria is quoted in the Australian edition of 'The Spectator' as describing TDS as a "hatred of President Trump so intense that it impairs people's judgement and has led to well-respected columnists describing him as a 'fascist', a 'white supremacist' and a 'Nazi'".

202. **Unconscious bias.** It is not only unacceptable to display or advocate politically incorrect language and behaviour – equally as bad is being guilty of unconscious bias. The Australian Public Service Commission warns against what is described as "unintended discrimination"; a situation where even though you never intended to cause offence you are guilty and need to be re-educated. The Commission's website includes research by the ANU that lists 150 examples of unconscious bias, including: stereotyping marginalised individuals and groups, defending the status quo, group think and confirmation bias. The Australian Taxation

Office also warns against "unconscious biases" where employees unconsciously discriminate against or cause offense to those who are LGBTIQ+, indigenous, culturally or linguistically diverse, mature age, disabled or because of gender.

203. **Vegan.** The Urban Dictionary describes a vegan as somebody "who slaughters and kills fruits and vegetables". Shareena Hamzah from the UK's Swansea University believes such is the popularity of veganism and vegetarianism that meat eating will soon be under threat; especially as it is so unhealthy and because it contributes to global warming. As a result Hamzah argues the language and expressions we use when referring to animals will change and she quotes a number of examples from the People for the Ethical Treatment of Animals (see Non-animalist language).

204. **Vegetative state.** Once used to describe people who are disabled to such a degree that they do not appear conscious and are unable to communicate; as in a recent newspaper article headed "Vegetative woman gives birth in care". Vegans consider the description offensive as it demeans vegetables and ignores the fact they are 'alive' and able to respond to their environment. Alternatives include "comatose" or "an individual of alternative, non-binary perception, communication and movement".

205. **Vertically challenged.** A non-judgemental term used to describe short people. For example "Snow White enjoyed the friendship and company of seven vertically challenged, no-gendered individuals" (See short shaming).

206. **Victim revisionism.** Involves the process whereby those self-identifying as victims rewrite the past to ensure their victim status is reaffirmed.

207. **Virtuous masculinity.** The American Pastor Jeff Sanders and drawing on the Bible describes a virtuous man as one who is a provider, a leader and someone who is able to earn respect and show compassion, integrity and faith.

208. **Virtue signalling.** The Urban Dictionary describes this as taking "a conspicuous but essentially useless action ostensibly to support a good cause but actually to show off how much more moral you are than everyone else". Businesses and corporations virtue signal by championing causes related to the environment, indigenous affairs and gender equality to disguise the fact their primary aim is to make a profit. An example involves the head of BHP, Andrew Mackenzie, arguing that fossil fuels represent an "existential risk" to the planet while his company continues to make millions in profit each year involving coal and petroleum.

209. **Western Civilisation.** Despite being responsible for developing a political and legal system that ensures freedom and liberty and guarantees human rights; initiating the industrial and digital revolutions; providing increased standards of living and initiating scientific and medical revolutions, Western civilisation has no right to be considered more beneficial or preferable to any other civilisation. Cultural-left critics argue to do so is to be guilty of white supremacism and Western essentialism (see whiteness).

Ignored, as argued by Steven Pinker in *Enlightenment Now: The Case For Reason, Science, Humanism And Progress*, is that not all cultures are equal and that Western civilisation, for all its flaws, deserves special recognition. Pinker argues that beginning with the Enlightenment and continuing with industrial, scientific and technological advances, Western civilisation is responsible for an unprecedented period of prosperity and growth that has improved the health and living standards of billions across the globe.

210. **Whiteness.** Dr Omid Tofighian from the University of Sydney condemns the traditional curriculum for enforcing 'whiteness'; defined as a curriculum that is Eurocentric, oppressive and complicit in denying the "identity and cultural background of marginalised groups". According to Tofighian subjects like history, literature, art and music must be radically overhauled as they are guilty of "racism, sexism, classism, historical

injustice and prejudice based on religion". (The Conversation website, 5th October 2015). The University of London's Collective argues that 'whiteness' promotes power and thought which is "racialized as white" and "heteropatriarchally/cisgenderly male". The University of the Sunshine Coast, under the heading of 'Race, Power and Privilege' as part of its 'Cultural Diversity and Inclusive Practice Toolkit', also criticises whiteness when arguing "Inequity, oppression and an imbalance of power are further entrenched by positioning 'white' as the reference point".

Paul T Le and Cheryl E Matais describe 'whiteness' as a "hegemonic racial dominance that has become so natural it is almost invisible". They suggest science education is not immune from the evils of 'whiteness' by arguing their research "identifies how whiteness operates in science education such that it falls short of its goal for cultural diversity". The South Australian curriculum also argues as science is a socio/cultural construct with no right to be considered preeminent that "Western science is the most dominant form of science but it is only one form among the sciences of the world" (See also Aboriginal and Torres Strait Islander Science).

211. **White supremacism.** A NSW school curriculum official cites the 'The Three Little Pigs' as an example of white supremacism. Instead of being an innocent children's story it "contains elements of a world view which the British authorities, if not all the convicts,

brought to Australia in 1788. The story assumes a society with private property and individualised labour. It applauds discipline and hard work and the solid stone or brick houses of Europe, it places non-material cultural pursuits second to material, and its primary motivation comes from fear of nature, or wilderness, in the form of a wolf. It could not be an Aboriginal folk tale or Dreaming story".

212. **White Privilege.** Those, through no fault of their own, who are of European and Anglo/Celtic descent are guilty of 'whiteness' as they are inherently privileged and guilty of oppressing and disadvantaging non-white victim groups. As such, they must be re-educated to ensure they are aware of their prejudices and atone for their sins – either conscious or unconscious. A guideline for the re-education of nurses and midwives guilty of 'whiteness' refers to adopting an approach that involves "a decolonising model of practice based on dialogue, communication, power sharing and negotiation, and the acknowledgment of white privilege".

A South Australian government department also asks employees to acknowledge white privilege when undertaking indigenous sensitivity training on the basis that "We seek to better recognise the influence colonisation and white privilege has (sic) on the department's internal and external interactions with Aboriginal people, their nations and communities, and guide opportunities for reconciliation into the future".

213. **Whitewashing.** Described as employing white actors and actresses to play the part of a non-white character, thus, further marginalising and oppressing people of colour. Ruby Hamad on the SBS website argues the lack of racial diversity in the media is a sign of prejudice. He writes "With Australia's default setting firmly set to 'white,' it is not surprising that in a social climate that still prioritises white voices, bigotry is on the rise".

214. **Woke.** Refers to being able define oneself and to see others and the wider world through a politically correct prism. The Urban Dictionary defines this as "A reference to how people should be aware in current affairs". As in "while you worried whether you could order a decaf, freetrade, almond milk latte China was building over 100 coal fired power stations, stay WOKE".

215. **Wokescold.** Involves being scolded and criticised for not being WOKE in relation to PC issues and debates. The American academic Rod Dreher recounts being attacked by a student after he praised the iconic photo of the sailor kissing the nurse in Times Square at the end of World War 11. The student argued it was a sexual assault and that the sailor "should have gone to jail".

216. **Women shaming.** See slut shaming.

217. **Yellow facing.** Similar to black facing and brown facing this is an example of cultural appropriation where a white person assumes the identity of an Asian. The

Melbourne comedian Cate Hanley Corley was forced to withdraw her comic act involving Aisha the Aussie Geisha from the 2019 Fringe Festival after an open letter signed by approximately 70 people criticised her. The letter argued Corley's act "borders on yellow face" as it "revolves around the belittling and insulting depiction of Asian peoples for cheap humour".

218. **Ze and zie .** A neutral, non-gendered pronoun used instead of 'he' or 'she', 'him' or 'her'. As in "The non-binary, gender free person told me zie will be here tomorrow".

POLITICAL CORRECTNESS AND THE CULTURAL-LEFT'S LONG MARCH THROUGH THE INSTITUTIONS

In the new order, Socialism will triumph by first capturing the culture via infiltration of schools, universities, churches and the media by transforming the consciousness of society.

Antonio Gramsci

POLITICAL CORRECTNESS: NO LONGER A LAUGHING MATTER

I first read about political correctness after buying a copy of *The Official Politically Correct Dictionary & Handbook* in 1993. The dictionary had been published in America and at the time the PC movement, while prevalent in America, had yet to achieve notoriety in Australia.

As I wrote all those years ago most of the examples in the

dictionary, authored by Henry Beard and Christopher Cerf, are humorous in nature and include examples like "vertically challenged" for small people and "chemically inconvenienced" for alcoholics. Other examples include "between jobs" for unemployed, "terminally inconvenienced" for dead and "motivationally dispossessed" for lazy.

Reading the American PC dictionary reminded me of a slogan being circulated when I was at La Trobe University during the 70s – 'Land Rights for Gay Whales'. This was a time when it was still possible to make fun of cultural-left icons and not be punished by authorities or vilified and attacked on social networking sites. Universities had yet to impose Diversity Toolkits to warn staff and students about what constituted politically incorrect language and nobody had heard of trigger warnings or Safe Spaces.

After reading more closely, though, and observing what was happening in Australia I discovered there is a dark side to political correctness as it was increasingly being used by the cultural-left to stifle discussion and debate and to enforce group think that made it impossible to disagree and to have an opposing opinion.

If you questioned the value of multiculturalism you were labelled a racist, if you argued there should be a cut in immigration the put down was you were xenophobic and if you were a man arguing it was OK for women to be feminine and alluring, the response was stop being so sexist.

As I wrote during the early 90s it was also true that in public life those who questioned or disagreed with what was politically correct were publicly vilified and in some cases in danger of losing their job. The late Fred Hollows, who spent his life alleviating the suffering of indigenous people suffering from blindness caused by cataracts, was condemned as homophobic for suggesting AIDS, when it first appeared in the West, was primarily associated with the gay community.

The historian Geoffrey Blainey who had achieved the standing of one of Australia's most eminent historians was pressured to leave his post at the University of Melbourne for daring to question the rate of Asian immigration. While not opposing immigration Blainey made the sensible point that if the rate was too high it would possibly lead to social unease and dislocation.

As discovered by the art historian Robert Hughes, it was also the case in the early 90s government style manuals became heavily influenced by political correctness. Hughes gave the example of the Federal Government's Style Manual in which words like 'sportsmanship', 'workman', 'statesmanlike' and 'craftsmanship' were considered unacceptable.

Similar to America, where the PC movement dramatically changed what was studied in subjects like literature, history, law and sociology, Australian universities also came under the influence of the cultural-left's campaign to overthrow the status quo by radically changing what was taught and how students and staff interacted.

Such was the increasing prevalence of political correctness that Ross Fitzgerald, who at the time was an Associate Professor at Griffith University, argued PC "was suppressing research, hijacking free speech and being enforced in a dangerously virulent way". At La Trobe University where I had studied the alternative student handbook pressured academics into becoming politically correct by attacking courses that students considered homophobic, racist or misogynist.

Pierre Ryckmans, the internationally famous sinologist who taught at both the Australian National University and The University of Sydney, went as far as arguing in his 1996 Boyer Lectures that universities had betrayed the primary reason for their existence. Ryckmans wrote "The main problem is not so much that the University as Western Civilisation knew it, is now virtually dead, but that its death has hardly registered in the consciousness of the public, and even the majority of academics themselves".

Fast forward to contemporary Australian society and Western societies in general and it's clear that political correctness now dominates and controls:

- how we are permitted to think and interact with others,
- what happens at work,
- how the print, electronic media and social networking sites present news and deal with issues,
- how language is used,
- what is taught in schools and universities, and

- how we are supposed to discuss and debate a range of issues, especially those related to gender and sexuality, the environment, multiculturalism, religion and the history and institutions associated with Western civilisation.

Proven by the vitriolic attacks on Margaret Court for arguing against the same-sex marriage legislation and the criticisms levelled at Israel Folau for condemning homosexuality, it's clear that anyone who dares to question politically correct orthodoxies is ripe for attack. Many argued that Court's name should be removed from the Margaret Court Arena where the Australian Open Tennis championships are held every year and Folau had his contract playing with the Australian Rugby team cancelled.

Another example of how dangerous political correctness is relates to the University of Western Australia, after initially agreeing, cancelling the contract to establish a centre managed by Bjorn Lomborg and based on his centre in Copenhagen. Critics of the proposed centre argued Lomborg failed to acknowledge the nature of the impending global crisis caused by man-made global warming.

Additional evidence of the destructive prevalence of political correctness were the vitriolic and poisonous attacks directed at the Australian cartoonist Bill Leak for having the honesty and courage to reveal the harsh reality about the dysfunctional nature of family life in many isolated Aboriginal communities. Leak's cartoon portrays an Aboriginal policeman with an Aboriginal child telling the child's father "You'll have to sit down and talk to your son about personal responsibility". The father replies "Yeah righto, what's his name then?". After drawing a cartoon that expresses a self-evident truth Leak was threatened with being taken before the Australian Human Rights Commission under Section 18c of the Racial Discrimination Act.

It is also no longer possible to celebrate and acknowledge the strengths and benefits of Western civilisation as the cultural-left argues all cultures are equal and there is nothing unique about the West. In the Australian national curriculum diversity and difference, the new code for multiculturalism, reign supreme as students are told cultural relativism prevails and all who migrate to Australia have the right to retain their customs, traditions and way of life.

The curriculum mandated for all Australian schools also adopts a postmodern interpretation of citizenship; one where instead of having an allegiance to Australia students are told "there are multiple perspectives of citizenship that reflect personal, social, spatial and temporal dimensions of citizenship". Students are also told "Individuals may identify with multiple 'citizenships' at any one point in time and over a period of time". Even though Christianity underpins our political and legal institutions and our parliaments begin with the Lord's Prayer the national civics curriculum also describes Australia as a "secular nation with a multi-faith and multi-cultural society".

Not surprisingly, given the impact of political correctness, the national curriculum privileges the history and culture of indigenous Australians to the detriment of Anglo/Celtic and

European Australians. For example, while Western civilisation and Judeo-Christianity are undermined and treated superficially students are told they must study the "unique identities of Aboriginal and Torres Strait Islander Peoples and how they shape national Australian identity" in all subjects from preparatory to year 10.

In its more extreme form, as previously mentioned, politically correct academics argue that subjects like history, literature, art and music must be radically overhauled as they are guilty of "racism, sexism, classism, historical injustice and prejudice based on religion". Western civilisation is guilty of promoting "whiteness" – defined as a "hegemonic racial dominance that has become so natural it is almost invisible".

In a 2018 edition of *English in Australia* (Volume 53, No 2), the national journal of the Australian Association for the Teaching of English, the argument is put that the way literature is taught is guilty of privileging heterosexuality and ignoring LGBTIQ+ perspectives and issues. As such the editorial argues English teachers should "make visible positive representations of diverse genders and sexualities". One paper argues in favour of "queering the curriculum and reading the curriculum in non-heteronormative ways" to ensure that what students encounter does not reinforce "heterosexual stereotypes, heterosexual privilege, the normalising of heterosexuality".

Such is the dominance of the political correctness movement in our universities that academics at both the Australian National University and the University of Sydney have refused attempts to establish a Western Civilisation Centre funded by a million-dollar bequest left by Paul Ramsay. In an open letter signed by 150 Sydney academics the argument is put that establishing a Ramsay Centre is guilty of promoting a "culturally essentialist and Eurocentric vision" of history and culture. In a more recent critique a number of Sydney University academics argue introducing courses funded under the Ramsay umbrella would be guilty of entrenching "a hard-right political agenda" calculated to impose a "narrow, masculinist, Anglocentric view of 'the West'".

Cultural-left academics argue teaching Western civilisation promotes an oppressive, heteronormative and sexist way of life that further oppresses already marginalised groups including: indigenous Australians, LGBTIQ+ people, non-European migrants and anyone else who is not white, heterosexual, middle class or financially well-off.

Radical feminist and gender theory represents an especially intrusive and one-sided example of political correctness impacting on schools, universities and Australian society at large. In 2004 in *Why Our Schools are Failing* I quoted a South Australian government curriculum document that argues gender is a social construct that has nothing to do with biology or chromosomes. It argues existing gender roles reflect inequitable and unjust "dominant power relation(s)" and that education must be directed at the "deconstruction and reconstruction" of such roles.

While the majority of parents are happy with the expectation that girls and boys celebrate their differences in a positive and beneficial way those in control of the gender-agenda disagree. Those supporting "heterosexuality as a norm" need to be re-educated and students must be taught to question traditional gender roles. One of the curriculum perspectives informing South Australian education is 'Gender perspectives', this is described as:

> *Gender perspectives, which recognise that gender is a social construction organised upon unequal power relations which define and limit opportunities for girls and boys (eg, men for public life and economic and political leadership, women for the domestic and care, the social capital). The current construction of the gender order also supports heterosexuality as the norm. Social constructions of advantage and disadvantage are of human making and therefore capable of change.*

Even though approximately 98% of Australians self-identify as female or male and an even greater percentage of babies are born either male or female the material associated with the Safe Schools gender and sexuality program also argues there is nothing normal or beneficial about heterosexuality. Those arguing sexuality is binary and, generally speaking, for the purpose of procreation are condemned as heteronormative and students are told they have the right to self-identify as whatever gender they are most comfortable with.

The radical, politically correct nature of Safe Schools is admitted by one of its creators Roz Ward who argues "only Marxism provides the theory and practice of genuine human liberation" and the "Safe Schools Coalition is about supporting gender and sexual diversity, not about stopping bullying". Leaving no doubt as to the program's real agenda Ward also suggests "It will only be through a revitalised class struggle and revolutionary change that we can hope for the liberation of LGBTI people".

Both Safe Schools and the Respectful Relationships program also present a very negative view of men and masculinity. The Respectful Relationships program that deals with domestic violence, while quite rightly stressing the appalling and unacceptable nature of violence against women, ignores that men also suffer as a result of domestic disputes and violence.

While contested, one figure suggests one in three victims of domestic violence are men and, such is the seriousness of the issue, that the Victorian Royal Commission into Family Violence recommends the government "take steps to identify and take account of the needs of male victims—including male children, older men who are victims of elder abuse by family members, and gay, bisexual and transgender men". Such is the power of the PC movement that it is rarely, if ever, admitted that domestic violence is especially prevalent in the gay community and among isolated indigenous communities.

To criticise the increasing prevalence of political correctness and the fact it stifles free and open discussion and debate is not an excuse for offensive language or rhetoric that targets and vilifies particular groups or individuals in society. Women should never be demeaned or treated as inferior, LGBTIQ+

people have every right to go about their business free of unfair discrimination and regardless of ethnicity or race all should be treated fairly and equally. Far-right organisations whether in the UK, Europe, America or Australia with their Nazi memes and bitter and violent rhetoric opposing immigration and denying the rights of non-whites, have no place in any civilised nation.

THE PAST IS A FOREIGN COUNTRY

With compliments to L. P. Hartley, the past is a foreign country and they do things differently there. Before the advent of political correctness growing up in working class Broadmeadows during the 50s and 60s, by comparison to recent times and for all its faults, was relatively straightforward and less complicated.

As a teenager with a violent, alcoholic father guilty of domestic violence I would be the first to admit that life was far from perfect growing up on a housing commission estate. There's no doubt that inequality and injustice existed. LGBTIQ+ people were not always treated fairly and many suffered violence from an unsympathetic and often callous society. Indigenous people and newly arrived migrants, especially if they could not speak English, were often discriminated against – as were women in relation to employment and education.

At the same time, Australia provided a relatively peaceful and prosperous environment where those willing to apply themselves, live by the laws of the land and work hard to achieve were able to succeed. It's also true that over the last 50 to 60 years much has been achieved in overcoming disadvantage and unfair discrimination.

While the cultural-left's politically correct narrative is that Australian society is riven with oppression, injustice and inequality the reality is that the Mabo decision affirmed indigenous land rights, same sex marriage is now legal, affirmative action plans for women are commonplace, the dangers of climate change are widely accepted and many corporations and businesses, instead of focusing on service delivery and maximising profit, are committed to virtue signalling by promoting politically correct causes. In response to the world-wide climate day strike held on Friday 20th September 2019 some 2100 Australian businesses according to *The Sydney Morning Herald* newspaper endorsed the strike as well as giving employees the opportunity to take action on the day. Even Andrew Mackenzie the CEO of the global resources company BHP, notwithstanding the companies investments in coal and oil, admits "global warming is indisputable" and "the global response does not yet match the severity of the threat".

The 60s was time of black and white TV, when tea was the drink of choice and no one had ever heard of cappuccinos or free trade, soy, decaf lattes. Bread came as white sliced or unsliced and families could only afford chicken once or twice a year. Long before the internet and mobile phones, red telephone boxes littered the suburbs and the majority of conversations occurred face to face.

While bohemians existed and books like George Johnson's *My Brother Jack* and the play *One Day of the Year* criticised and satirised Australian culture and way of life the overwhelming majority of people believed post-war Australia was the lucky country and there was much to celebrate, enjoy and respect. Politically correct concepts like 'identity politics' and 'victimhood' were unheard of.

Multiculturalism was yet to become the new orthodoxy and it was OK to be patriotic. Post Second World War migrants were expected to adopt to the Australian way of life, students took the oath of allegiance and saluted the flag at school assembly, parents told their children that they should be seen and not heard and people rarely took offence if they were the butt of the occasional sarcastic remark or joke.

My favourites at the time were: "How do you confuse an Irishman? Put two shovels in the corner and tell him to take his pick" and "How many gears does an Italian tank have – 3 reverse and 1 forward – 1 forward in case they are attacked from the rear".

Many Saturday afternoons were spent at the movies with a bag of Jaffas watching adventure films where actors like John Wayne, Alan Ladd and Errol Flynn played the hero - always brave and resourceful and capable of winning the day. A time, as admired by the American feminist author Camille Paglia, when actresses like Lauren Bacall and Marilyn Monroe were capable of being confident and independent while still being alluring and feminine.

This was also a time when kids were free range, rode their bikes without helmets, swam in creeks unattended and helicopter parents wrapping their children in cotton wool did not exist. Unlike today's generations of snowflake children we were also expected to be resilient and willing to take risks. Trampolines never had safety nets and parents never drove their children or accompanied them to and from school.

Growing up in a newly established suburb with childhood friends from Germany, Greece, Scotland, England, China, the Ukraine and Albania nobody talked of differences in ethnicity or race as we were all treated equally and happy to be Aussie kids. Loving Australia and acknowledging the benefits and strengths of our Western heritage were not crimes and in the cinema we were expected to stand and sing the then national anthem 'God save the Queen'.

The men went to work, came home and expected dinner on the table and the majority of women were more than happy to be wives and mothers. This was a time before radical feminism disparaged motherhood and argued the only way for women to succeed was if they became professionals and were successful in breaking the glass ceiling.

Civility and politeness were the order of the day with men giving up their seats on trams and trains to women and the elderly and where men were expected to be courteous to women by walking on the side of the foot path nearest to the curb.

Before the advent of the digital age, e-readers and the internet parents showed their children picture books, read classic fairy tales that are now criticised as sexist, misogynist and racist and it was common for students to visit the school library on a regular basis. Unlike many of today's children I devoured hundreds of books written by authors including H. G. Wells,

John Wyndham, Edgar Rice Burroughs and Ian Fleming.

Greek and Norse myths and fables like *The Iliad* and *The Odyssey* and *Beowulf* taught me about bravery and heroism and how, despite challenges and setbacks, it is possible to overcome adversity and win the day. *Sinbad the Sailor*, Kipling's *Kim* and the *Arabian Nights* introduced me to strange and exotic lands where human nature was portrayed in a vivid and compelling way.

Parables and stories from the *Bible* taught me about the nature of good and evil, how temptation and sin betray us all in different ways and that love, generosity and kindness are better than being ego centred, narcissistic and consumed by materialism. I also learned we are all made in God's image, regardless of race, gender or ethnicity and that all are entitled to liberty, freedom and equality. As quoted in the King James' version of the Bible "There is neither Jew nor Greek, there is neither bond nor free, there is neither male nor female: for ye are all one in Christ Jesus".

School teachers were respected, discipline was strict and classroom noise and misbehaviour were rare notwithstanding many classes had over 40 students. We were expected to work hard, focus on our studies and if we were not up to the required standard were told that near enough was not good enough and failed. Instead of today's progressive, new-age classes where teachers are 'facilitators' and 'guides by the side', teachers were in control and while classes were often interactive and collaborative the focus was on mastering the basics and the essential knowledge, understanding and skills associated with key subjects. Thankfully, we also had technical and high schools on the basis that not everyone has the same abilities, motivation or interests and there was nothing wrong with a trade as a career.

Unlike today's politically correct approach to education where the first time students are challenged by a competitive, high risk test or examination is in Year 12 students were often streamed in terms of ability and progressing through high school required gaining your Proficiency, Intermediate, Leaving and Matriculation certificates. Students also failed subjects and even though I eventually found academic success I remember as a student failing French and Mathematics B in Form 4 (Year 10), Mathematics 1 in Form 5 (Year 11) and Economics in my Matriculation Year (Year 12).

School reports were also kept to a minimum with each student given a numerical grade or percentage and ranked against others in the class. Unlike today's PC descriptive reports that go for pages and confuse parents with jargon and edubabble when I was a student parents were given a succinct, easy to understand and clear assessment of their child's progress – or lack of progress!

In Victorian schools what were called the *Australian Readers* were widespread based on the belief that all primary and secondary students needed to be familiar with those fiction and non-fiction stories, events and poems that together ensured students were culturally literate.

Literature, while including Australian poets and authors, introduced students to literary classics involving Chaucer, Shakespeare, Keats, Shelley, Wordsworth, Austen, Dickens and more recent authors and poets including Arthur Miller, T. S. Eliot, Bertolt Brecht, Chekov and Tolstoy. Such literature, instead of being deconstructed in terms of power relationships according to the dictates of cultural-left theory, also dealt with existential questions about what constitutes right and wrong, how best to find fulfilment and how best to deal with life's challenges. Literature also was valued for its moral and aesthetic character and for dealing with universal themes exploring human nature in an illuminating, persuasive and convincing way.

In history we learned about the key events, dates, people and movements associated with Western civilisation that could be traced back through the rise of representative government and universal franchise, the impact of colonial expansion, the industrial revolution to the Enlightenment, the Reformation, the Renaissance and the heritage associated with Judeo-Christianity, ancient Rome and Greece and the rise of the Sumerian civilisation.

While drawing on a range of other cultures, including what is now China and the Middle East, such a narrative recognised that Australia was part of the Anglosphere – those countries where English is the dominant language and where the political and legal institutions evolved from a Westminster parliamentary system and English common law. On the world map printed on the back of our exercise books those countries associated with the British Empire covered the globe from east to west and north to south. The expression 'the sun never set on the British Empire' was more than just a figure of speech.

Of course, it is impossible to return to what is often depicted as a glorified past and there is much about the 50s and 60s that was unacceptable. At the same time it is vital to appreciate that we can only fully understand the present and better chart the future if we know about the past. As argued by T. S. Eliot, continuity is equally as important as change and to refuse to recognise and to deny the value of what has gone before is an example of arrogance that leads to cultural amnesia. In Australian history, for example, it is wrong to adopt a 'black armband' view and to ignore the attempts to ameliorate indigenous disadvantage and the steady progress made over the last 40 to 50 years.

THE IMPOSITION OF POLITICALLY CORRECT LANGUAGE AND GROUP THINK

The neo-Marxist, post-modernist faithful who over 40 years ago proposed a Long March through the enfeebled cultural and educational institutions of the West have possibly succeeded beyond their wildest dreams in Australia.

Giles Auty, *Culture At Crisis Point*.

As highlighted in George Orwell's novel *1984* language and how it is used influences how we think and act and controlling language is a key strategy employed by totalitarian regimes of the left and the right to manipulate people and enforce groupthink. In Orwell's dystopian novel what is described as Newspeak leads to a situation where "thoughtcrime" is impossible as "there will be no words in which to express it".

The slogan "War is Peace, Freedom is Slavery, Ignorance is Strength" best illustrates how Big Brother subjugates citizens by radically altering the meaning of words and, as a result, controlling their ability to think rationally and independently. Such is the insidious evil of distorting language to control how people think that Orwell writes:

> *The implied objective of this line of thought is a nightmare world in which the Leader, or some ruling clique, controls not only the future but the past ... If he says that two and two are five — well, two and two are five. This prospect frightens me much more than bombs.*

The slogan employed during the same-sex marriage debate "Love is Love" is also an example of politically correct language use. Taken on face value such a statement appears reasonable and beyond dispute – all should be free to love whoever they choose and the State has no right to decide otherwise. A closer reflection, though, suggests that not all types of love are the same or that they should be treated equally.

The love between a woman and a man that culminates in marriage and the possibility of procreation is heterosexual in nature and throughout history and in most cultures is considered preeminent. The love between a man and a man or a woman and a woman is clearly not the same type of love.

Similarly, the love a parent has for a child or the type of love between siblings is also very different to the love between a wife and a husband.

While the cultural-left's use of politically correct language is widespread and now dominates public and private discourse it should be noted that using language to persuade and convince has been evident since the time of the ancient Greek philosophers and sophists. What is called rhetoric, both verbal and written, includes devices such as:

- emotive language,
- euphemisms,
- attacking the person,
- appealing to expert opinion and facts,
- employing logic and reason and
- basing one's argument on personal experience.

It also should be noted that employing rhetoric is not restricted to the cultural-left. During America's involvement in the Vietnam war the military used the expression 'collateral damage' to describe innocent civilians being injured or killed and 'friendly fire' when its soldiers were the victims of American firepower. Forcefully removing peasants from their farms and villages, instead of being described for what it actually was, was labelled 'pacification'.

Notwithstanding rhetorical devices are common across the political spectrum what distinguishes political correctness from other forms of argument and language use is that:

- it is a strategy associated primarily with the cultural-left,
- while originating as an off shoot of Marxist theory it has since morphed into a rainbow alliance of

cultural-left theories including: Neo-Marxism, feminism, postmodernism, deconstruction and LGBTQI+, post-colonial and gender and sexuality theories,
- Western civilisation, capitalism and the free market, Judeo-Christianity, marriage between a woman and a man and heterosexuality are its chief enemies,
- identity politics prevails where so-called disadvantaged individuals and groups, such as women, LGBTIQ+ and indigenous people and those of colour and non-European ethnicity and culture, are always presented as victims made powerless by an oppressive system,
- rather than relying on reason and rationality (as such concepts are Eurocentric, phallocentric and binary) arguments are subjective and relative in nature and based on emotion, and
- the intention is to challenge what is condemned as the status quo and to mandate a new-age, politically correct utopia where diversity and difference reign supreme, all are equal and free of discrimination (unless you are a white, older, Christian Eurocentric male) and individuals are empowered and no longer constrained by the past and the obsolete institutions associated with Western civilisation.

Recent events involving Australia's universities illustrate the success of the cultural-left's political correctness movement in influencing and controlling how people communicate, think and interact with one another. In language much like that of Big Brother in *1984* the University of Sydney proudly proclaims the purpose of education is to "unlearn". On the basis that "not everyone has been taught how to unlearn" the university exhorts students to "challenge the established, demolish social norms" in areas such as same-sex marriage, indigenous land rights, peace studies, refugees and the environment.

Monash University, the University of NSW and Flinders University have Diversity Toolkits and Inclusivity Guidelines that tell academics and students what to say and what to think instead of promoting open discussion and dialogue. When teaching and dealing with students, academics are told they should:

- celebrate diversity and difference (except for those misguided students "who see themselves as part of the dominant culture" and who might react against being told all cultures are equal and worthy of respect,
- be careful not to espouse "heteronormativity" and "heterosexism", and
- describe Australia as "invaded" and not suggest at the time of the First Fleet that indigenous peoples were "primitive" or "native".

Ignored, unlike Aboriginal and Torres Strait Islander cultures at the time of the First Fleet, is that Western civilisation was characterised by:

- complex forms of irrigation, husbandry and agriculture,
- the printing press,
- advanced political and legal systems,
- cities and roads that housed millions,
- explorers and navigators who had circumnavigated

- the globe and
- the adoption of technology and science that led to steam engines, telescopes, microscopes and the rudimentary beginnings of modern sanitation, hygiene and medicine.

And while there is no doubt that Western civilisation drew on and made use of discoveries and scientific innovations taken from Chinese and Islamic cultures the reality is that it is only in the West that civilisation achieved so much in terms of material, scientific, technological and social progress.

Also ignored by those academics opposed to establishing a Ramsay Centre for Western Civilisation is that Western culture, instead of reinforcing "existing power relations and privilege", is responsible for establishing universities in the first place and for championing academic freedom as the basis for rigorous and impartial intellectual debate.

Monash University's 'Inclusive Language Guide' provides another example of how advocates of political correctness have taken the long march through the institutions. On the basis that "language is enormously powerful and politically charged" the guide suggests using 'workforce' instead of 'manpower' and 'artificial' instead of 'manmade'.

Australian universities also have Safe Spaces where Muslims, women, LGBTIQ+ and indigenous students are guaranteed a secure and safe environment free from supposedly hostile white, heteronormative and racist students. As three Queensland 'white' students found out when they entered a computer centre reserved for indigenous students and subsequently complained about their treatment on a social networking site, retribution soon follows those who transgress.

In addition to having to spend thousands of dollars defending themselves against a complaint of being racist bought under section 18c of the Racial Discrimination Act the students also faced being publicly criticised for simply expressing a valid point of view.

Trigger warnings are also increasingly prevalent where vulnerable students are warned beforehand if they are about to encounter supposedly offensive or challenging texts or other material. Examples include literature that deals with homosexuality, violence, rape, death, racism or mental illness. Literary texts such as *Macbeth* (violence and murder), the play *Medea* (where children are killed) and novels like *The Man Who Loved Children* (where someone commits suicide) are decidedly problematic and offensive.

Governments, local councils and companies like Qantas are also involved in promoting PC language. The Victorian government's inclusive language guide criticises the relationship between men and women on the basis that "Heteronormativity is the assumption that everyone is heterosexual (straight), and that this is the norm" and "heterosexism is the belief that non-heteronormative sexual orientations or gender identities are unnatural".

As previously stated, the fact that approximately 98 per cent of Australians self-identify as male or female and that the natural order of things is for men and women to procreate to ensure the survival of humanity is ignored. Also ignored, as doctors and nurses well know, is that the physiology of the human body is better suited to a heterosexual relationship.

How literature is taught at Sydney University also adopts a decidedly postmodern, politically correct approach. Instead of the Western culture's literary canon, students learn about "the rise of identity politics, the culture wars and queer theory". Under the heading "postcolonial modernisms/modernities" students learn how "race, gender, class, sexuality, nation and religion shape ideas of being modern".

If classic texts such as Shakespeare's tragedies are studied students are made to 'deconstruct' them in terms of power relationships involving the new trinity of gender, ethnicity and class. A third subject involves deconstructing "text-production as a social and ideological act", where students consider the "ideological influences impacting on theoretical discourse about language and textuality".

This politically correct view of literature is the opposite to that associated with a liberal view of education; one where literature is studied for its moral and aesthetic significance and value. Instead of appreciating how language is employed and crafted or what a literary work suggests about what it means to be human and how we relate to the others and the wider world the focus is on deconstructing texts in terms of critical theory. It should also be noted that much of literature, including Blake's poems, novels by Dickens and plays by Brecht, instead of reinforcing the status quo present a critique of Western civilisation and the Church.

THE BRAVE NEW WORLD OF POLITICAL CORRECTNESS

Those defending political correctness often argue it is a form of politeness and civility and that it is beneficial as it pressures people to treat others with fairness and respect. There is an element of truth in such an argument as some language and belief systems are deeply offensive and it is clearly wrong to vilify and denigrate others because of who they are or their way of life.

At the same time the reality is that political correctness is underpinned by radical, cultural-left ideology and can be traced back to Marxism and what is known as critical theory. And central to the left's long march is the decision to take control of the education system and to ensure what is taught and what students learn champions cultural-left ideology. As detailed in a quotation attributed to Gramsci:

> *The first step in emancipating oneself from political and social slavery is that of freeing the mind. I put forward this new idea: popular schooling should be placed under the control of the great workers' unions. The problem of education is the most important.*

It is no accident that Roz Ward justifies Safe Schools in terms of Marxist ideology or that much of the sociology of education portrays schools and education as servants of capitalism –

describing them as an essential part of the ideological state apparatus used to reinforce the power of the elites and to further disadvantage those, such as the working class, women and people of colour, already oppressed.

Since Friedrich Engels and Karl Marx published *The Communist Manifesto* in 1848 and wrote "workers of the world unite!" communism has been one of the most powerful and influential ideologies shaping world history. Whether the Russian revolution and the rise of the USSR as a world power or the impact of communism in China, South East Asia and South America communism has impacted on the lives of countless millions of people.

Central to communism is the ideal "from each according to their ability, to each according to their needs" and the belief that capitalist societies, the right to own private property and to make a profit are inherently unjust and oppressive. If the revolution is to succeed then the workers must overthrow the status quo and take control of the state apparatus and the modes and means of production. And as proven by what happened under Stalin in the USSR and Mao in China, if violence and terror are what is required to achieve the workers' paradise, then the end will always justify the means.

As noted by the Italian intellectual Augusto del Noce when discussing the significance of Wilhelm Reich's *The Sexual Revolution* the total lack of any moral or ethical underpinning leads to a situation where "every kind of violence, every ruse, every illegal action, every dissimulation, and every deception become licit if they are deemed to be necessary to reach the goal... politics absorbs morality within itself, and it would seem that there could not be a more radical violation of the traditional moral code". In this Machiavellian world of political and social action there is no right or wrong based on what is ethical or morally good, there is simply the desire to gain power for power's sake.

In China, as a result, during Mao's reign of terror over 50 million Chinese died because of starvation, torture and execution. And as so clearly illustrated in George Orwell's *Animal Farm* while communism and its comrade in arms socialism begin with the promise of equality and freedom for all they quickly descend into violence and oppression where those in charge impose a totalitarian regime. A regime in many ways worse than what the revolution replaced.

Under Stalin millions also died, starved and were imprisoned and citizens faced a bleak and barren life compared to those in the West where capitalism and liberalism ensured prosperity and a standard of living far beyond what communism could ever provide. In Cambodia under Pol Pot's reign of terror approximately two million died, the country was bankrupted and those who survived lived in daily terror. Cuba and Venezuela provide other examples of how oppressive and inhumane communism is as the individual liberties and rights we take for granted and as our birthright are denied.

As noted by Michael Gove in a previous quotation it is possible to trace the origins of the cultural-left's political correctness movement to a number of Marxist intellectuals and academics associated with what has become known as the Frankfurt School established in Germany during the 1920s. In addition to becoming dissatisfied with communism these intellectuals also realised such was the prosperity and freedom experienced by those living in the West there was little, if any, chance of the disaffected storming the barricades and using violence to take control.

As such, they shifted the focus of the revolution from the economy to what has become known as the 'culture wars'. Gove describes this as a time when in order to overthrow the status quo and radically change society the focus had to be "less and less on workers' struggles and instead (become) engaged in wider battles". Gove especially notes the rise of identity politics as a result of what is often described as the long march through the institutions. Augusto del Noce makes a similar point when arguing "It is clear that what today is called the left fights less and less in terms of class warfare, and more and more in terms of 'warfare against repression'". Whether this supposed repression is caused by Western societies being Eurocentric, homophobic, sexist, heteronormative or misogynist the fight to overthrow capitalist society is now focused on winning the culture wars.

One of the most significant theories associated with the Frankfurt School is critical theory – defined by the Stanford Encyclopedia of Philosophy as a liberating and emancipatory philosophy directed at "decreasing domination and increasing freedom in all its forms". Whether freeing those oppressed by capitalism, racism, sexism or a heteronormative, binary sense of gender and sexuality the purpose of critical theory is overthrow the status quo and to initiate a new period of equality and freedom for all.

The Encyclopedia goes on the suggest that in order to qualify as 'critical theory' what is being advocated "must explain what is wrong with current social reality, identify the actors to change it, and provide both clear norms for criticism and achievable practical goals for social transformation". As with communism the emphasis is very much on social transformation on the basis that existing capitalist societies are rife with injustice and inequality.

It is impossible to underestimate the impact of critical theory on universities and schools in subjects like sociology, history, literature, geography, science and politics. As previously mentioned, literary texts are now critiqued in terms of power relationships associated with gender, ethnicity and class and history no longer deals with the overarching narrative associated with the rise and evolution of Western civilisation.

Gove also makes the point that the cultural revolution of the mid to late 1960s saw a rebirth of critical theory as a significant and powerful force for radical change. Illustrated by the 1968 student riots in Paris, Woodstock and the counter-culture movement, the emergence of radical feminism, gender and LGBTIQ+ theories this was a time, as Wordsworth observed about the French Revolution of 1789, "glorious was it to be alive, but to be young was very heaven".

While there is no doubt that aspects of Western culture and the institutions and way of life associated with it were, and still are, in need of critique and improvement what occurred represented a far more radical and destructive attack.

As noted by the Giles Auty in *Culture At Crisis Point,* the cultural revolution represented a significant and far reaching social, intellectual and cultural change that attacked and undermined the very foundations of Western societies.

> *What 'the long march' has attempted is not just the overthrow of Western culture in a narrow sense but a rewriting of the*

> *moral and civil codes which underwrite the entire God-inspired history of Western civilisation.*

The American author Roger Kimball is his book *The Long March* also suggests that the cultural revolution of the late 60s signified a dramatic and far reaching change in the way the cultural-left sought to radically remake society in its image. Kimball writes in relation to America in particular "In a democratic society such as ours, where free elections are guaranteed, political revolution is almost unthinkable in practical terms. Consequently, utopian attempts to transform society have been channeled into cultural and moral life".

Whether the anti-war movement and race riots, student activism on campus, the sexual revolution brought about by the birth control pill and a Dionysian culture of immediate physical gratification, the end result was that long held and accepted beliefs and institutions were attacked and undermined. The concept of Western culture being beneficial or preferable was also a target of the cultural-left's long march through the institutions. As noted by Arthur M. Schlesinger, Jr this was a time when:

> *The Western tradition, in this view, is inherently racist, sexist, "classist", hegemonic; irredeemably repressive, irredeemably oppressive. The spread of Western culture is due not to any innate quality but simply to the spread of Western power.*

Schlesinger also makes the point that for all its faults and shortcomings compared to other cultures Western civilisation contains within itself the ability to identify and critique its flaws and injustices and to move towards greater freedom, equality and justice for all.

> *There remains a crucial difference between the Western tradition and the others. The crimes committed by the West have produced their own antidotes. They have produced great movements to end slavery, to raise the status of women, to abolish torture, to combat racism, to defend freedom of inquiry and expression, to advance personal liberty and human rights.*

While politically incorrect to criticise or find fault in indigenous cultures the truth is that many were, and still are, characterised by practices such as child brides, slavery and the exploitation and subjugation of women. And there are still countries like Saudi Arabia, Brunei and the United Arab Emirates that embrace a fundamentalist view of Islam were practices like female circumcision, the victimisation of LGBTIQ+ people and treating women as inferior are prevalent and considered acceptable.

POLITICAL CORRECTNESS AND ITS IMPACT ON SCHOOLS

In the long march through the institutions, reforms must be sought that satisfy the immediate needs of students, teachers, and parents. Pie-in-the-sky politics must be rejected in favour of a program of revolutionary reforms built around such issues as democracy, free classrooms, open enrollment, adequate financial aid for needy students, and development of a critical antidiscriminatory and socialist content of education.

Bowles and Gintis, *Schooling in Capitalist America*

The previous quotation exemplifies how the cultural-left defines the purpose of education; one where the curriculum and how schools are managed and organised is directed at overthrowing the status quo and heralding a socialist inspired utopia. Opposing this ideological approach is a liberal view of education. An education that is concerned with the formation of character and that can be traced back to the ancient Roman and Greek philosophers.

A liberal education is one where knowledge is inherently worthwhile and that to be educated is to be familiar with those disciplines and areas of knowledge that constitute a well-balanced, comprehensive and rigorous experience. While evolving and growing over the years (the curriculum is no longer restricted to Latin, Greek, Grammar, Rhetoric and Logic) schools generally introduce students to a defined body of knowledge, understanding and skills and a particular disposition and way of seeking understanding and truth. Professor Brian Crittenden in *Cultural Pluralism and Common Curriculum* defines this liberal view of education as:

> *... in effect, a systematic and sustained introduction to those public forms of meaning in which the standards of human excellence in the intellectual, moral and aesthetic domains are expressed and critically investigated.*

The English poet and inspector of schools Matthew Arnold's phrase "the best that has been thought and said" is often referred to when suggesting what constitutes a worthwhile and beneficial education. And it should be noted that critics generally ignore the second half of what Arnold argued; that it is vital to turn "fresh and free thought upon our stock habits and notions". Cultural conservatism is as much about change and evolution as it is about acknowledging and holding on to what has gone before.

The Victorian 'Blackburn Report' argues in a similar way when suggesting that all students are entitled to encounter "our best validated knowledge and artistic achievements". In arguing such is necessary the 'Blackburn Report' has much in common with classical Marxism as advocated by the Italian Antonio Gramsci and his belief that peasants, if they were to be truly liberated and able to overthrow capitalism, must be educated. In *Selections from the Prison Notebooks* Gramsci speaks favourably about learning Latin and Greek and the benefits of an education centred on "the interior development of personality, the formation of character by means of the absorption and assimilation of the whole cultural past of modern European civilisation".

In their seminal book *Schooling in Capitalist America* the two American academics previously quoted present one of the most direct attacks on a liberal view of education. Instead of schools and what is taught being inherently worthwhile or beneficial they argue "inequities in education are part of the capitalist system and are likely to persist as long as capitalism survives". Building on a Marxist critique of society the argument is that schools are a critical part of the 'ideological state apparatus' that reproduces inequality and indoctrinates future citizens to accept their subservient role.

While individuals might believe that they are free and in control of their destiny and that education is a worthwhile pursuit they only do so because they have been conditioned and are victims of false consciousness. Meritocracy, competition and focusing on academic studies are all tools employed by capitalist society to strengthen and reproduce itself.

Drawing on Marxist and cultural-left inspired intellectuals including Pierre Bourdieu, Michael W. Apple, M. F. D. Young, Louise Althusser and in Australia Bob Connell and Bill Hannan this radical attack on the schools has had a profound effect. Joan Kirner, the one-time Victorian Minister for Education and Premier, champions this Marxist inspired view of education in a speech given at a conference organised by the Victorian Fabian Society in 1983. Kirner argues:

> *If we are egalitarian in our intention we have to reshape education so that is part of the socialist struggle for equality, participation and social change, rather than an instrument for the capitalist system.*

As such, equality of opportunity must be replaced by equality of outcomes; a situation where positive discrimination is needed to ensure so-called victim groups and the disadvantaged no longer suffer because of an elitist and oppressive education system.

One of the most strident and effective advocates of a cultural-left view of education and the relationship between schools and society is the Australian Education Union (AEU) and one of its predecessors the Australian Teachers' Federation (ATF). Since the mid to late 60s both organisations have argued against the academic curriculum, competitive examinations, standardised literacy and numeracy testing and government funding for non-government schools. The ATF's 1985 curriculum policy describes Australian society as one characterised by:

- *The pronounced inequality in the distribution of social, economic, cultural and political resources and power between social groups, which restricts the life development of many.*

- *The role of the economy, the sexual division of labour, the dominant culture and the education system in reproducing inequality.*

It should not surprise the Australian Education Union, in addition to arguing that schools must be radically overhauled, advocates a politically correct ideology in areas such as: the environment, indigenous affairs, multiculturalism, refugees, gender and sexuality, funding non-government schools and Australia's involvement in the Iraqi war after the 9/11 attacks in America.

The AEU's 2003 'Policy on gay, lesbian, bisexual and transgender people' argues Australian society and its institutions, including schools and churches, promote homophobia and heterosexism and schools have a major role to play in advancing the rights of GLBT people. The policy also states it is wrong to believe that there is anything "natural" or "normal" about heterosexual sex and relationships and that "All curriculum should be written in non-heterosexist language" and that "homosexuality and bisexuality need to be normalised".

The union, in order to justify its policy in related material, argues 9-11% of the population identify as exclusively same sex attracted and another 10% of the population identify as Bi-Sexual. The paper concludes "Thus at any one stage 20% of the population would not identify with a heterosexual lifestyle"

Ignored, as previously mentioned, is that according to a national survey carried out by La Trobe University academics approximately 98% of Australians surveyed identify as either women or men. In a second national survey published in the Australian and New Zealand Journal of Public Health (Vol 27, No 2) involving 10,173 men and 9,134 women the results also disprove the exaggerated claims made by those seeking to normalise LGBTIQ+ lifestyles. In this second survey 97.4% of men and 97.7% of women identify as heterosexual.

The teacher union's opposition to the Howard government's decision to support America in the Iraqi invasion after 9/11 also displays a cultural-left perspective. In a media release dated 17 January 2003 the union argues that there is "absolutely no justification" for the invasion and that the Howard Government is guilty of promoting "militarism and xenophobia". In a second media release, dated 20 March, the Australian Education Union argues against the "illegal invasion of Iraq" and teachers are urged to "support students who take anti-war stance" and to "encourage participation in peaceful protests with the support and involvement of other family members".

More recently the AEU has been a consistent and vocal supporter of primary and secondary students taking time off school to attend a series of national climate-day strikes generally held during the school week on a Friday. The AEU President Correna Haythorpe in a media release dated 8 March 2019 states "The AEU supports the democratic right of students to take direct action, giving voice to their real concerns about the impacts of climate change, and protesting the inaction by the federal government." In the educational jargon much loved by PC educators Haythorpe goes on to say "Our students must be equipped with the right skills to become innovators and agents of change in a rapidly changing world" and "Climate change is a reality and the only acceptable debate is about how we deal with the consequences and ensure that our children and students are prepared for the future."

Even though approximately 34% of Australian students attend

non-government schools (20% Catholic and 14% independent) and the major political parties support parental choice and government funding the AEU also adopts a politically correct approach to choice and diversity in education. The union has a long history of opposing the existence of non-government schools evidenced by a 1985 policy document that describes such schools as "selective rather than comprehensive with many devoted to the social elite".

The union goes on to argue the "dual system of schooling is a pronounced cause of inequalities of educational outcomes" and that "the resource efforts of government should be wholly devoted to the public systems which are open to all". Ignored is the existence, especially in Sydney, of selective government schools that are not open to all students and the fact that not all parents are able to afford the cost of expensive real estate in the enrolment zones of many academically successful government schools.

More recently, in its response to the 2011 Gonski review of school funding and in subsequent debates about what constitutes a fair and equitable funding system, the AEU continues its opposition to governments financially supporting Catholic and independent schools:

> *Although substantial government funding to private schools has become entrenched in Australia in recent decades, we believe there is no pre-existing, pre-determined entitlement to public funding; i.e. there is no a priori justification for public funding to private schools.*

How English is defined and taught as a subject provides further evidence of how successful the cultural-left has been in enforcing its ideology on schools. With reading and how students are expected to respond to literature, drawing originally on the works of the South American Marxist Paulo Freire, the focus is very much on what is described a 'critical literacy'.

Freire condemns the more traditional approach to teaching English as "massification" – a situation where instead of thinking critically and independently students are forced to acquiesce to the process and be submissive. Practices like rote learning, teachers as experts and failing to address real-life issues are also criticised as promoting a "banking concept" where learners, supposedly, are passive and treated as empty vessels waiting to be filled with knowledge.

Critical literacy, on the other hand and much like critical theory, argues that learning a language and education more broadly must be emancipatory and liberating. Drawing on Marxist theory Freire argues the true purpose of education is to allow students "to perceive themselves in dialectical relationship with their social reality... to assume an increasingly critical attitude toward the world and so to transform it".

Within Australia academics in charge of teacher education and professional bodies like the Australian Association for the Teaching of English and the Australian Curriculum Studies Association are staunch supporters of Freire's work and the concept of critical literacy. Two influential academics Walton and Luke, after noting the importance of Freire's work at a conference held at Griffith University in 1992, suggest that

> One of the recurring themes which emerged from the discussions and plenaries was the need to critique and re-work Freirian approaches to critical literacy, particularly in the light of feminist, poststructuralist and socially-based linguistics.

An editorial written for a 2004 edition of *English in Australia*, bemoaning the re-election of the conservative Howard Commonwealth Government, also illustrates how pervasive this Marxist inspired approach to English is. The author, Wayne Sawyer, argues teachers had failed to adequately teach critical literacy and that teachers must redouble their efforts as John Howard being re-elected as Prime Minister proved students were easily duped and not able to think clearly. Sawyer argues:

> *My main concern is with what the election tells us about our profession. English for the last ten years – not least on the pages of this journal – has trumpeted the cause of critical literacy ... What does it mean for us and our ability to create a questioning, critical generation that those who brought us balaclava'd security guards, Alsations and Patrick's Stevedoring could declare themselves the representatives of the workers and be supported by the electorate?*

Critical literacy and associated feminist, gender, sexuality and post-colonial theories have also had, and continue to have, a significant impact on how literature as a school subject is now taught.

Literature before the cultural-left's campaign to take control was generally restricted to those novels, short stories, plays and poems that had something significant, profound and lasting to say about human nature, how people interact and relate to the wider world and how we perceive and cope with the myriad challenges and issues we have to deal with as we journey through life. As D. H. Lawrence suggests in an essay titled 'Morality and the Novel' the "business of art is to reveal the relation between man and his circumambient universe at the living moment". Good literature was also acknowledged and celebrated as the finest example of language use and where words, whether written or spoken, were crafted in such a way as to be evocative, memorable and exemplary.

Literature, especially Greek, Roman, Celtic and Norse myths, fables and legends, also deals with the predicaments, heroes, archetypes and feelings that underpin much of Western culture and that speak to our inner emotional and spiritual selves. Such archetypes and myths deal with love, betrayal, courage, sorrow, forgiveness and the need to find a more spiritual and transcendent sense of meaning in what is an often unforgiving, transient and challenging world. The stories and exploits of legendary heroines like Athena and Aphrodite and heroes like Odysseus, Beowulf and Thor still resonate today as evidenced by Hollywood movies like 'Clash of the Titans', 'Wonder Women', 'Thor: Ragnarok' and the television series 'Vikings'. The Bible is also centre place in dealing with what it means to be human and how best to lead the good life in a world characterised as a vale of tears.

Instead of focusing on the moral and aesthetic importance of literature, one where students learn to understand human nature and to empathise with others, the emphasis is now on deconstructing so-called texts in terms of power relationships and critical theory. In a paper delivered at a AATE National Conference Maria Pallotta-Chiaarolli argues that the English classroom must be re-positioned as "a site of deconstructionist and interventionist strategies when challenging/resisting dominant discourses of marginalistaion and prejudice". Examples of prejudice include: "homophobia, heterosexism and AIDS-discrimination" along with "racism, ethnocentrism, classism and sexism".

In a paper published by the American National Council of Teachers of English the argument is put that Shakespeare's *Romeo and Juliet* is in danger of reinforcing "heterosexist and misogynist messages" as it ignores the fact that "not all people are heterosexual or conform to traditional gender roles". As a result of critical literacy Conrad's *Heart of Darkness* is also criticised because of its treatment of slavery, *Moby Dick* as it centres on killing whales and Mark Twain's *Huckleberry Finn* because it includes the word "nigger".

The campaign to redefine literature even extends to children's books where *Little Black Sambo* is politically incorrect as it disparages people of colour, *Thomas the Tank Engine* because it has a hierarchy of trains with the Fat Controller (the capitalist boss) in charge and *Cinderella* and *Snow White* because they reinforce a patriarchal view of the world where women are subservient to men and the happy ending is defined as a heterosexual marriage.

How history is taught in schools has also been dramatically redefined to make it politically correct. While no one is suggesting that schools and the curriculum should embrace an overly celebratory and positive approach, what Geoffrey Blainey describes as a "three cheers view of history", there is mounting evidence that what students are presented with unfairly undermines and critiques both Western civilisation and Australia's foundation as a penal colony and its evolution since 1788. As detailed by Stuart Macintyre in *The History Wars* more radical approaches emerged during the heady days of the Vietnam war moratoriums and the rise of the counter-culture movement. How Australian history was taught was especially affected:

> In the 1960s and 1970s, critical approaches to Australian history questioned established interpretations of settlement and progress. Historians pursued voices frequently absent from the national narrative. Social historians of feminist, migrant and Aboriginal perspectives challenged the exclusiveness of traditional historical approaches.

This was a time when the grand narrative associated with the rise and development of Western civilisation increasingly came under attack as academics turned towards what Macintyre describes as "history from below" involving Marxist, feminist, gender and post-colonial theories. As a result historians shifted the focus of history teaching to incorporate the treatment and perspectives of indigenous Australians, gays and lesbians, recently arrived migrants and women.

How history is detailed in the Australian national curriculum from preparatory to year 10 illustrates how successful the cultural-left has been in redefining the subject. Similar to the other subjects, students are told in the history curriculum that Australia is a multicultural, secular society characterised by diversity and difference and where various cultures, ethnic and race groups interact and live. Even though Australia owes much to Western civilisation, Judeo-Christianity and enlightenment values like rationality and reason the curriculum promotes a relativistic stance where all cultures and histories are treated equally and deserving of recognition and respect.

Three of the cross-curricula priorities that inform history, in addition to other subjects, are Aboriginal and Torres Strait Islander Histories and Cultures, Sustainability and Asia and Australia's Engagement with Asia. While there are literally hundreds of references to indigenous history, culture and spirituality the impact and significance of Western civilisation and Judeo-Christianity is treated in a superficial and fragmented fashion. Christianity is rarely, if ever, mentioned and while the dark side of Western civilisation is emphasised (including slavery, mistreatment of women, the stolen generation, mandatory detention and the civil rights movement both in Australia and America) indigenous culture and history are presented in a positive light and beyond reproach.

In relation to Asia, and similar to the way indigenous culture and history is treated, students are presented with a sanitised picture. A picture that ignores and air brushes from history the millions starved, tortured and killed under dictators like Mao, Pol Pot and Ho Chi Minh. Whereas Australia is a Westminster, parliamentary democracy where people's rights and freedoms are protected there is also no mention in the national curriculum that the majority of Asian countries are totalitarian, single party regimes where property can be confiscated and people imprisoned and denied the rights we take for granted without any protection or recourse.

One of the recommendations of the 2014 national curriculum review I co-chaired argued there should be a greater focus on "the contribution of Western civilisation (and) our Judeo-Christian heritage". In response Michael Kindler in Curriculum Perspectives Vol 35, No 1 April 2015 argues:

> *Many Australians do not have a Western, so termed "Judeo-Christian heritage". Such a recommendation ignores the multicultural, multi-faith composition of contemporary Australia, and recommends privileging one over another, when a pluralist would recognise that one interpretation of civilisation and its heritage should stand equally and alongside any other.*

Cultural relativism and identity politics prevail ignoring the reality that Australia's political and legal institutions and much of our language, literature, music and art are inherited from Europe, Ireland and the United Kingdom. While the numbers are diminishing it's also true that Australia's mainstream religion is Christianity.

POLITICAL CORRECTNESS AND ITS IMPACT ON UNIVERSITIES

The philosophy of the school room in one generation will be the philosophy of government in the next.
Abraham Lincoln.

Universities, as a result of the 60s and 70s cultural revolution and the decision by the cultural-left to take the long march through the institutions, have especially been affected by politically correct ideology. As previously mentioned, the opposition to establishing a centre for Western civilisation funded by the late Paul Ramsay best illustrates the current state of affairs. The fact that so many academics oppose the centre on the basis that it is guilty of promoting a supposedly Eurocentric, patriarchal, misogynist and white interpretation of history is a clear example of groupthink and an unwillingness to even consider other points of view.

Similar to the school curriculum, historically a university education has centred on a liberal education; one that has its origins in Europe and the United Kingdom and that can be traced back to ancient Greece and philosophers like Aristotle, Socrates and Plato. Such an education as argued by Cardinal Newman in *The Idea of a University* inculcates a particular habit of mind involving "freedom, equitableness, calmness, moderation, and wisdom; or what in a previous discourse I have ventured to call a philosophical habit". As previously noted, the English poet T. S. Eliot in *Notes Towards a Definition of Culture* argues in a similar vein when suggesting universities "should stand for the preservation of learning, for the pursuit of truth, and in so far as men are capable of it, the attainment of wisdom".

A liberal education is not immediately utilitarian or concerned with enforcing a particular ideology or political philosophy. As noted by the American academic, Israel Scheffler, in 'Reflections on Educational Relevance', a balanced, objective and impartial education must be allowed to:

> *... facilitate independent evaluation of social practice... as instruments of insight and criticism, standing apart from current social conceptions and serving autonomous ideals of inquiry and truth.*

Such has been the destructive impact of the cultural-left's takeover of universities that Pierre Ryckmans, a sinologist who taught at the Australian National University and The University of Sydney, argues that the liberal concept of a university no longer exists. In his 1996 Boyer Lectures 'The View from the Bridge' Ryckmans describes a young academic attacking a visiting speaker for his "narrow bourgeois elitism" for daring to discuss the importance of Chines literati painting.

In addition to rehashing slogans made popular by Mao's cultural revolution the young academic argues it is impossible to discriminate or be objective as all value judgements are relative and subjective. Ryckman's replies "to deny the existence of objective values is to deprive the university of its spiritual means of operation". As previously noted, such is his distaste and hostility to what a university education has been reduced to that Ryckmans concludes:

> *The main problem is not so much that the University as Western civilization knew it, is now dead, but that its death has hardly registered in the consciousness of the public, and even the majority of academics themselves.*

Ryckmans is not alone in his pessimistic and disturbing summation of the impact of cultural-left ideology and the deleterious impact of critical theory and its more recent progeny.

Merv Bendle, a Senior Lecturer in History and Communication

at James Cook University, also criticises the subservience to cultural-left theories and criticises Australian academics for their "simplistic default position of class, sex, race" and for uncritically advocating "politically correct positions which are widely shared and immune to criticism". When detailing what he sees as the unremitting attacks on Western culture caused by "an ideological contagion of shame and self-loathing" ('The Suicide of the West', *Quadrant* October 17, 2016) Bendle argues this "nihilistic worldview is now institutionalized throughout Western academia". In relation to Australia Bendle argues this bleak view, drawing on existentialism to deconstructionism, "has been systematically promoted throughout academia, the schools and the media".

John Carroll, formally at La Trobe University, puts a similar case when arguing that Australia's cultural elites, including universities, the school curricula, museums and art galleries, no longer are committed to rationality and objectivity exemplified by "the Western tradition since classical Greece". Carroll argues in 'How I became a political conservative' (*Quadrant* May 9, 2015):

> *The Left impulse has been less calmly quizzical, more aggressively hostile, seeking to undermine existing authorities without replacing them. Accordingly, art has to be shocking; values have to be deconstructed; meanings have to be exposed as rationalisations for entrenched wealth and privilege.*

The British art critic and academic, Giles Auty who now lives in Australia, also condemns the cultural-left's takeover of the academy and the pernicious influence of what he describes as postmodernism and its close relative political correctness. Auty describes postmodernism as "a deeply anti-democratic political as well as a cultural movement". One that constitutes "leftist totalitarianism by stealth" and that is now rampant in our schools and universities. As a result Auty concludes in 'How the West is Really Being Lost' (*Quadrant Online* 29 June 2018) :

> *The widespread politicisation of culture and the arts in Australia has had a particularly unfortunate effect on all kinds of aesthetic judgments, which are widely dismissed today as elements of an outdated bourgeois Western culture.*

RADICAL GENDER AND SEXUALITY THEORY

Since the Frankfurt School championed critical theory as a way to critique and demolish capitalism and to herald the new socialist utopia a rainbow alliance of related theories has entered the culture wars. In addition to neo-Marxism, feminism and post-colonial theories radical gender and sexuality theories have also had a significant and ongoing impact on society, schools, universities, and institutions like marriage.

As previously mentioned one of the most egregious examples of gender theory is the Safe Schools program championed by Roz Ward when she was an academic at La Trobe University in the Australian Research Centre in Sex, Health and Society. Ward has made no secret of her conviction that promoting a radical LGBTIQ+ theory of gender and sexuality on school children is one way to bring about a new world order of sexual liberation and freedom. As previously quoted, Ward argues "It will only be through a revitalised class struggle and revolutionary change that we can hope for the liberation of LGBTIQ+ people".

Central to this battle is redefining gender and sexuality as social constructs instead of a biological imperative and a scientific fact. The material endorsed by the Safe Schools Coalition argues that gender and sexuality are fluid concepts and criticises heterosexism as a binary, oppressive concept. Students as young as 8 and 10 are told to celebrate diversity and difference on the basis "there are many genders beyond 'male' or 'female'; gender can be fluid or limitless" and that "There are no rules about who you can be: all you need to do is be yourself". The definition of being LGBTIQ+ is based on self-identification and has nothing to do with one's sex at birth.

The bias evident in the Safe Schools Coalition program is further illustrated by its claim that the program is justified because 15.7% of students are either same sex attracted, gender diverse, trans or intersex ('Stand Out' – Safe Schools Coalition). Ignored is the research demonstrating that heterosexuality is the norm and that while LGBTIQ+ people should never be unfairly discriminated against they are a small minority of the population.

Research carried out by Anthony Smith and Paul Badcock from La Trobe University conclude approximately 98 percent of men and women aged 16-59 identify as heterosexual. In the survey only 1.6 per cent of men identify as gay and 0.9 as bisexual while 0.8 of women describe themselves as lesbian and 1.4 as bisexual. In a paper published in *People and Place* Vol 12, No 4, 2004 Shaun Wilson writes:

> *This paper confirms earlier research estimating the GBLT population at around two per cent of the Australian adult population with higher numbers of gay and bisexual men than lesbian and bisexual women.*

Professor Patrick Parkinson from the University of Queensland also concludes that the overwhelming majority of the population in Australia and the United Sates is heterosexual. He writes "Large scale surveys in recent years (when homosexual orientation has become normalised and therefore much less likely to be a matter which people fail to disclose) put the figures on same-sex attraction in the adult population as between 1% to 3%.

Also ignored is the research showing, notwithstanding that puberty and adolescence are a time of experimentation and anxiety about gender and sexuality (thus suggesting the behaviour might be more widespread), that by the time adolescents pass through puberty and reach adulthood many are happy to be male or female.

The La Trobe University's Australian Research Centre in Sex, Health and Society is one of the principal supporters of the Safe Schools Coalition and is responsible for a resource titled 'The Practical Guide to Love, Sex and Relationships'. Similar to the Safe Schools Program the material advocates a strong LGBTIQ+ agenda that argues society is guilty of enforcing a Eurocentric and heteronormative view of gender; one that impacts negatively on boys and girls.

One of the activities titled 'Freedom Fighters' asks students to role play a situation where Martians invade and enforce a destructive binary code - where boys are boys and girls are girls. Students are then asked to be freedom fighters where the 'male' hero sings:

> *You don't have to be a certain way just because you have a penis*
> *You don't have to be a certain way just because you have a vagina*
> *We're not gonna care about that*
> *We're gonna do what we wanna do*
> *We're gonna be who we wanna be*
> *I'm gonna lead you guys to victory and then I'm gonna go home and enjoy my collection of vintage*

dolls
Because we're free, damn it
And they may take our penises
They may take our vaginas
But they will never take our freedom!

WHAT'S TO BE DONE?

The first step in countering the destructive and poisonous influence of political correctness is to call it out and reveal its true nature. While disguised as the need to be courteous and polite and not unfairly criticise others political correctness is a virulent and oppressive form of thought control and group think. Whether by corrupting language or enforcing cultural-left ideology on issues like gender and sexuality, immigration, multiculturalism, Judeo-Christianity or the significance of Western civilisation the purpose is to radically reshape society in its image.

Underlying political correctness is the impact of critical theory that can be traced back to the cultural revolution of the late 60s and before then the establishment of the Frankfurt School in Germany in the 1920s. Realising there was no chance of a revolution in the West, as had occurred in Russia under Lenin, Marxist academics argued the way to success was to take the long march through the institutions. Best illustrated by Gramsci's quotation previously referred to, the focus is on capturing and radically transforming society by targeting institutions like schools, universities, churches and the media.

The cultural-left is also able to achieve its goals by arguing any change is minor and incremental in nature, thus, disguising the often radical and extreme nature of what is intended. Same sex marriage, when first championed by the cultural-left, simply involved changing the definition to include gays and lesbians but it now encompasses the full range of LGBTIQ+ people as well as initiating a wider campaign to normalise radical gender and sexuality theories in the school curriculum. Faith-based schools, in particular, are now being pressured to adopt staffing and enrolment policies that run counter to the religious beliefs such schools are called upon to uphold.

The second step is to learn from the success of the political correctness movement and to adapt its strategies where relevant and useful. Adopting a medium to long term view is critical as is the need to formulate well defined strategies; including engaging in the battle of ideas in the public arena as well as universities, schools, the workplace and in one's private life. One of the defining differences between the cultural-left and those more conservative is the Left's ability to appoint advocates and fellow travellers to key positions in professional bodies, unions, educational organisations and tertiary institutions.

In relation to education it's no secret that those imbued with cultural-left ideology and group think either gain or are appointed to senior and influential positions across key organisations, including: the Australian Curriculum Assessment and Reporting Authority, the Australian Curriculum Studies Association, the Australian Education Union, the Deans of Education and many of the state and territory equivalent bodies. Similar to the old industrial relations club, the way educational policy in areas like the national curriculum is developed involves a small coterie of like-minded individuals all intent on maximising their influence. For many years now education in Australia has been the victim of what the NSW academic Ken Gannicott describes as 'provider capture'. To say silent is to acquiesce and to vacate the field is to allow the cultural-left to dominate and win control.

The third step is to mobilise and organise like-minded individuals and organisations who are aware of the dangers of the political correctness movement and who are willing and able to join the public battle of ideas. In America groups of like-minded academics opposed to political correctness like the Heterodox Academy and the National Association of Scholars provide a lightning rod for those opposed to cultural-left ideology and a vehicle to express both opposition and to articulate what needs to be championed.

Reasserting the primacy of reason, rationality and logic and highlighting the irrational and dangerous nature of political correctness represents the fourth step. To suggest all cultures are equal is to adopt a relativistic position where it is impossible to argue female genital mutilation and child brides are unacceptable. The reality is that Western culture, with its commitment to liberty, freedom and the inherent dignity of the person, is superior to uncivilised cultures where inequality, injustice and violence are widespread and entrenched. One of the key reasons so many millions of refugees risk their lives to reach Europe, the UK, Australia and the United States of America is because they seek the prosperity and liberty denied in their own lands.

The argument that words have no agreed meaning, that knowledge is a social construct based on power relationships and that there are no truths leads to either silence, epistemological suicide or adjudicating truth claims by resorting to violence. As argued by Michael Casey from the P. M. Glynn Institute in his book *Meaninglessness*:

> *If everything – language, morality, custom, culture, and human life itself – is nothing more than what it is described to be from time to time, then everything is subordinate to and forever in the service of power, to be made and remade at whim.*

Such is the extreme and bizarre nature of the political correctness movement it is also vital to be able to laugh and to reveal that the emperor has no clothes. As proven by the late Bill Leak and his son Johannes, humour and satire are key weapons against the thought-police intent on stifling debate and enforcing sterile group think. Arguing it is politically incorrect to order a short black coffee as it might offend people of colour or that Santa Claus can no longer say "Ho, Ho, Ho" because it might be mistaken for the American slang for a prostitute is ridiculous. And anyone who has read Swift's 'A Modest Proposal' detailing how to solve the Irish problem during the famine will appreciate the power of satire in calling out cant and hypocrisy.

www.ingramcontent.com/pod-product-compliance
Ingram Content Group UK Ltd.
Pitfield, Milton Keynes, MK11 3LW, UK
UKHW021326180426
11947UKWH00017B/1469